Disaster

Prologue:

Some poets believe the night sky is a black tapestry of salt stars. This makes it two-dimensional, when really that blackness above our heads is depthless, reaching out thousands of years to grab pocketfuls of light and sprinkle them into our view. I've always found comfort in how stars only show themselves at night, forgetting they lay just unseen in the daylight. There's something so pure about that abyssal blackness and their twinkling counterparts. How far did that light travel through endless, unaccompanied space to land on my retinas? I wonder if sometimes we only think of the night sky as a dark template for something else to shine, instead of gazing at that foreverness between the lights.

My fascination with stars began when I was born into the night sky, too eager to gaze at that dazzling canopy to wait for the hospital. When I was young, I'd stick my fat fist up in the air, squint one eye, and close my hand around a juicy star. When my fingers uncurled and I found them unsalted, I merely worked up the excitement to plunge back into the sky, and try again. It wasn't until much later that I discovered stars really can peel themselves away from that tapestry. But the only thing in my hand was the heaviness of the place they once were. Old French and Latin teamed up to describe this very feeling, using the root *astor* for star, and *dis-* meaning "without".

So it's only fitting that when I overflowed with that cosmic heaviness and fell plummeting to the earth, the word out of everyone's mouth was disaster.

Chapter 1

"Why did you do it?"

The question almost makes me smile. Almost. I'm not so careless to let it slip out, spill my true thoughts with even the slightest twitch. No, my face is smooth as marble. Unreadable. To anyone else, it would look unnerving, but Dr. Wilson sees it for what it is. A calculated move in a game of chess. *Psychological* chess, with a *psychiatrist*. The high stakes only make me more determined. Ok, and more afraid.

"Why is that such a popular question? That must be three times in four days. Surely you have a satisfactory answer by now?" I look at him directly, reflecting the careful scrutiny in his eyes. He returns my stare, then smiles. There's a hint of amusement in that smile.

"I would like to hear it from you, if that's alright?" A request disguised as a question. I decide to use his smile against him. Wielding a head tilt, I give off an air of faux curiosity. A small wrinkle moves in between my eyebrows to match.

"Why did I try to kill myself? That's what you're asking?" I drip the faintest bit of uncertainty in my voice. "Then why are you smiling?"

Still he stares. I can feel my cheeks start to burn under

his gaze. His eyes are so piercing, so examining that I move my gaze, looking over his shoulder instead. Dr. Wilson lets the silence settle, making me want to squirm. Still I sit, wearing calmness like armor. Beneath my shirt, my heart is hammering.

He ignores the question, saying instead, "Willow, you look very uncomfortable. What are you afraid of?" His face exudes friendliness and trust. He seems so genuine I almost open my mouth and tell him. Instead, I construct a disposition of natural calmness and boredom. Fear? That has to be good guesswork. There's no way I *look* afraid. I stifle the temptation to wipe my palms on the sweatpants I'm donning, doubting the gesture would be missed.

I consider my options. Being truthful is definitely *not* plausible, and outright denial is just as condemning. I try casual indifference, maybe a hint of boredom. A bland, emotionless reply. "I'm sorry to have given that impression, but I'm not nervous. I'm just tired of answering the same questions." I give a small sigh. "Sure, the first time wasn't easy, but now it's a bit annoying. If the answer is important, it's probably been written down."

They write everything down, all of these types of places do. What you eat. How many times it took to wake you up (7:30am!). Your mood on a scale of 1-10. If you've whined enough about yourself. The other kids here are professional whiners, some wearing tears like pearls, others more reluctant to share. But they all do in the end. Their heads crack open, and out comes the good stuff, their memories, their poor family dynamics, how they feel about all of it. In the end, everyone gets cracked open like an egg, and they stain the carpet with confession.

But that won't happen to me. That *can't* happen. I have too much to hide, too much to lose. And that smile, that *stupid smile* tells me maybe Dr. Wilson knows it too. He knows this is high-stakes chess, and the way his eyes are pinched with focus makes me feel like he's seeing five moves ahead. All I'm focused on is getting through this intake.

He tips his head down, raises his eyebrows, and says, "If you're sure." But underneath the measured words, his subtext screams *do you really want to play this game?*

Did I mention I've never played chess?

We finish intake and a nurse comes in to show me to my room. I stand to leave and he does too, chuckling softly and shaking his head. "This is going to be fun, isn't it?" Without reply, I turn and walk out the door, wiping the sweat from my palms.

Chapter 2

I get a room to myself, which is a bonus. I don't know anyone here, but I know the types well enough to feel relief at not having a roommate. The Stoic, the Cryer, the person who, for the life of them, just *can't stop talking*. The tragically broken pretty girl. The guy with anger issues. The rest are just garden variety crazies. Count me in with the latter.

The room is small, a few drawers for clothes, a desk and bathroom hugging each other, and a twin bed on the opposite wall. Everything is either white or in calming shades of blue. I deem it offensively inoffensive.

All my stuff is on my bed, already having been searched. I scan the pile and notice my phone is missing, but everything else seems to be in order, including a journal I don't recognize. Opening it, I find tiny, loopy writing on the inside cover.

Willow,

I picked you up this journal so you could write some of your thoughts down. I spoke with Dr. Wilson, and he agrees it could help you get better and hopefully get you home sooner! We'll have our first family session on Thursday with Dr. Webber. It'll be a conference call since I can't fly down there. Can't wait to hear your voice! Keep your head up.

Love, Mom

The spine cracks as I close it and fall back into the bed. There's no way I'm going to use it, but it was thoughtful nonetheless. Today is Monday, giving me three days before family therapy. I close my eyes, but a soft knock on the doorframe tells me my 15-minute settling in window has officially closed. The same nurse, Amanda, I think, smiles from the doorway. "Willow," she says, "why don't you come join us in the common area? It'll be good for you to get to know some of your peers." Peers. Patients. Psychologically unstable, hormonally-filled teenagers locked together in the same building.

Sure, sounds like a picnic.

I close my eyes again before speaking. "That sounds like a great idea, but I'm pretty tired. I had to catch an early flight this morning to get here." The lie rolls off my tongue, and I press my palms to my eyes to cement it. Technically I did fly down, right after getting discharged from the hospital, but I'm not wiped out from sitting on a plane for three hours.

And don't get me wrong, I really *am* tired, complete with brain fog and muscle-cramping weariness. My official label is depression, with a sprinkle of self-harm and a splash of suicidal ideation for funsies. At first they thought it was SAD, you know, Seasonal Affective Disorder? But that must have been too ironic, so they stuck me with the big, bad, Major Depressive Disorder instead. I'm basically a steaming cup of lethargy.

On cue my stomach rumbles, as if it would like nothing more than to be filled with liquid exhaustion. I wait for Amanda to leave but feel the foot of my bed sink in. I so dearly want to roll my eyes. "That sounds like an exhausting morning! Unfortunately, we don't like our depressed patients to be by themselves too much. Depression loves to make us feel isolated and alone," Amanda comments, like there's a person just hovering over my shoulder. Like she didn't just use the royal "us" instead of "you". I wait a minute, trying to think of a counter. Silence eats up the seconds.

The bed springs back up, and I think she might be leaving. When I open my eyes, she's a couple feet away with one foot facing the bed and one foot toward the door. Amanda throws me a smile, motions for me to get out of bed, and continues, "Come on, get up! I promise you'll feel better once you're up and talking to people. You can even help me make some friends since I'm new here too!" Like I'm a kid.

Or just really broken.

I close my eyes briefly and sit up. This place is *ridiculous*. When she sees me getting up, her smile widens even more. This. *Place*. The smiles and positivity and optimism are nauseating. I get to the door quickly to save her face from breaking, and we walk down the hallway dotted with doors to the common area. Two kindergarteners arm in arm on a mission for friends.

Oh yes, Dr. Wilson. What fun.

After promptly ditching Amanda, I'm acquainted with a blond girl called Zena (the tragic beauty), a tall guy with short, choppy red hair and lots of freckles named Emerson (a fellow depressive), a guy just taller than me with dark skin and fiery eyes named Samson, *not* Sam (anger issues), and a larger girl with wild brown hair who introduces herself as Piper, category pending. Piper has a loud, barking laugh that swivels heads and a dozen or so shallow, healing cuts she wears with pride. I glance down at my long-sleeved shirt and baggy sweats; I can't even imagine going without these protective layers. There are three other patients I've lost names to, two boys and one girl, so I sit with Emerson and Zena as the minutes tick down till the next group.

The common area is medium-sized with a large wall of windows adjacent to the nurse's station. There is a ping-pong table (paddles and ball by request), a piano, and a variety of old couches and plush chairs to fill the space. A TV shares a wall with the Nutrition room, which is just large enough to accommodate the snacks sent by parents and a juice machine. There's a whiteboard across from the nurse's station that has the daily schedule and all our individual appointments, and I see "Psychotherapy Group" is scheduled to start in five minutes. I turn to Emerson nervously and ask, "Psychotherapy Group? What's that about?"

"Dr. Patin runs it. She's one of the therapists," he explains. "It's pretty much talk therapy. People talk about why they're here, how their families suck, that sort of thing." I stare at him for a moment and feel my pulse quicken under my skin.

Egg cracking group, in other words.

He must see my anxiety and shakes his head, "It's really not too bad. You're new here, so she'll ask you a few questions, but no one really expects you to open up on the first day."

Emerson shoots me a reaffirming smile, and I nod. Under my skin, my muscles twitch, antsy at the thought of being stuck in a room and sitting for an *hour* while secrets are painfully extracted from unwilling participants.

Before the silence can get too long, they call us in to group, which is in a small, stuffy room just off the common area. It's adorned with plush chairs and worn couches, the walls decorated with horrifically cheesy quotes like "Just breathe" and "You are enough!" I sink into a squashy, red chair and smooth my palms against my pants. Looking around, I see a few other people with the same, standard issue sweatpants. A couple people brought blankets, while others fidget with things in their laps: silly putty, stress balls, and what looks like a plastic jar filled with water and glitter. Of course it isn't glass.

Across from me Samson glares at the carpet as the door swings open and a lady, probably in her mid 30's, walks in and smiles at all of us before taking a seat on a straight-backed, plastic chair. As if someone cast a spell over the room, her presence brings an abrupt end to the chatter.

She crosses her ankles and smooths the hem of her skirt before launching into the session. "Good afternoon! Is everyone comfortable and ready for group?" She sounds like an airline attendant, telling us all to bring our tray tables and seats into the upright and locked position. I wait for her to tell me where the emergency exit is, but she plows ahead. Beside me, Zena rolls her eyes. "If anyone missed it on the whiteboard, today's group is Psychotherapy." She scans us all until her eyes land on me, then smiles. "We have a new member in our community joining us today. Could anyone tell Willow the rules for group?"

The girl whose name I don't know brushes a few strands of long, brown hair from her eyes and speaks up. "Basically, don't be mean or judgmental, try not to compare yourself or one-up other people, and just be respectful." She moves her hand, and the curtains of hair fall back over her face.

"Thank you, Hazel. Any questions?" Dr. Patin addresses me, and when I shake my head she clasps her hands together. "Alright. Let's all go around and introduce ourselves and share one fun fact. Willow, would you like to start?" Another request disguised as a question.

I nod and—what the heck—give a smile, wide with irony. "Well, I'm Willow. Fun fact? I'm from Michigan." I make sure to give a neutral, demographic fact, and relevant since this prison is in northern Utah. Glenview Memorial Psychiatric hospital, home of the crazies. On my right, Zena introduces herself and says that she's a twin. Samson shares that he plays, make that played, on his school's varsity soccer team. I wonder what happened.

In less than two minutes, everyone has gone and the room falls quiet again. I can practically hear each person hold their breath and stare avidly at the carpet, which now I see has a large stain in the middle. I study it fervently while we wait.

It turns out to be exactly what Emerson predicted. Matt, short with big, round, blue eyes, is the focus of the beginning. He tells us all, seemingly against his better judgement, how his dad doesn't understand his anxiety. Apparently Matt lives alone with his dad, who works multiple jobs to keep them afloat. He makes a couple of references to drug use, but doesn't say much about it. The comments about his dad make Jeremy, the other guy I couldn't place, give the slightest shake of his head, and Dr. Patin pounces.

"Jeremy? How do you feel about what Matt said?" His eyes freeze for a moment before he composes himself.

"Well, that sounds really awful, but I guess I can't relate." An encouraging nod from Dr. Patin forces him onward. "My parents are more of the smothering type. I mean I'm 16, and they still won't let me drive. They completely *lost it* when they found out I'd been using." A few other people around the circle give small nods, including Zena and Piper.

    I start wondering if I'm the only one here who has never done drugs when Piper says, "I mean I definitely didn't want them to react badly, like what you're saying Jeremy, but when they saw the cuts, they blew me off. Totally ignored it. *Some sort of reaction would have been nice*." She adds an afterthought, "Not that I was doing it for attention or anything."

    At the mention of cutting, I'm pulled into my memories. It's hard to believe *that moment* happened only a few days ago. There wasn't much I could do to prevent it, seeing as I was in a short-sleeved scrub top. The memory flickers across my thoughts like black and white film, soundless.

    In one frame is my mom with her hands pressed against her mouth, her eyes wide with horror. I can see her freeze, the gasp caught in her throat. I cast my eyes from her silent trauma. The next frame my dad stands beside the bed, staring at my skin, just staring. His face was the same except for the tiniest head shake. The same one I've come to know is filled with disappointment. Not fear or sadness or shock. I crossed my arms, burned through with shame.

    Suddenly, I'm aware all the talking has stopped. I look up to see eight pairs of eyes swiveled in my direction. Dr.

Patin's face is all sympathy. "Willow, you seemed lost there for a moment. What were you thinking?"

My brain goes into high gear, frantically fabricating lies. "Um, nothing. I guess I just zoned out for a second."

"Have you ever self-harmed?" I can see the others sit up a little in their chairs.

"Technically yes, but it was just once, and a long time ago." Lie. I do my best to convey the truth. Relaxed posture. Open palms. I don't think she buys it.

"And what about your parents? How did they find out?" Against my protesting, my cheeks start to burn. My body language says *believe me*, but my body says *it's a load of BS*. I'll need to work on that.

"Oh, I was washing the dishes and my mom saw. We talked about it after, and it really wasn't a big deal. I haven't *self-harmed* since," I answer, careful to use her choice of words. How many lies was that? A pause unfurls into the space, and no one is eager to fill it. I thought it all sounded fairly benign, but now I'm not as sure. Thankfully Dr. Patin moves on, checking back in with Matt. I can feel my muscles unconsciously relax, and the remaining ten minutes pass unceremoniously.

When Dr. Patin announces we are free to leave, I don't try to conceal my relief as I walk-run out of the room. Emerson catches up with me in the common area and tells me I did alright. "Thanks," I say, "that was more draining than I thought it would be. I think I'm going to go catch up on some sleep."

He frowns slightly. "Yea, psychotherapy group is one of the worst; the rest aren't so bad. I'd be careful about sleeping though," Emerson adds, "If they think you're spending too much time in your room, they'll put you on room restriction."

Room restriction? This. Freaking. Place. I smile in thanks. "Oh, right. Well, I'll see you later." He throws a hand up as a goodbye, and I walk back down the hallway. I'm filled with an odd relief when I arrive at my room and find it unlocked. That has to be a good sign, right? Remembering that they do fifteen minute checks with us newbies, I glance at the clock on my nightstand. If they see me journaling, then maybe they'll feel differently about me being alone. I set the journal and a dull golf pencil (courtesy of Glenview Memorial) on my desk, then turn back to the room.

I lay down on the floor between the bathroom and my bed with my knees bent and feet flat on the ground. Exercise, they say, is a wonder drug for depression. As a former runner, I'd have to agree. Not that you'd be able to tell these legs ever did more than sit and waste, based on the state of them now.

I crank out rapid-fire sit-ups. After 100 I start on push-ups. I use the nightstand clock to time a few planks. Sit-ups, push-ups, planks. Rinse and repeat until my arms are shaking and they finally give way. With a sudden jolt I see the fifteen minutes has elapsed.

I drag myself up and slide into the desk chair right as a nurse knock on the door frame. "Just doing checks. You alright? A couple of your friends were asking about you." Friends? The people I've known for all of six hours?

I manage a weak smile. "Yea, I'm great. Just had some thoughts I wanted to get down," I say, gesturing to the notepad.

The nurse introduces himself as Anthony and gives a half shrug. "Alright. Well if you need anything, just let me know." He pushes off the doorframe and disappears back down the hall. In case anyone else comes this way, I walk to the door and close it quietly before starting on rounds of jumping-jacks, squats, and lunges.

Some ancient civilizations believed in sweating the sickness out of people. As my muscles tire and salty tears make their way down my face, I can't help but feeling like they may have been on to something. The more tired I become, the more the thing inside of me loosens. All I can feel is my ragged breathing and my muscles screaming in protest and my legs wavering. I can't feel that black, tarry thing inside me or the terror pulsing in my veins at being in a psychiatric hospital. I can't feel the ache for being home, the freezing, unrelenting hopelessness, or the pain that landed me here in the first place. With every grunt of effort, I sweat all of it out.

It isn't long before I can't feel a thing.

Chapter 3

The daily routine drags on so much, I let out a small sigh when it's finally Thursday. Every morning they come in and wake me up for breakfast, but honestly, who can eat at 7:45? I usually just grumble something incoherent and try to fall back asleep, but so far I'm zero for three.

There's a morning group at 9:00 where people set goals for the day, clearly wading through the remnants of sleep-med fog. Yesterday I skipped this morning torture too, considering it far too early to properly dissect my psyche. I decide to skip today as well. I got a few comments from the nurses, but no one seemed bothered by it. I'm hoping this morning will be no different.

I've been using the breakfast and group time do come up with new workouts, which wake me up far better than early morning brain-yoga. I'm not exactly sure yet how the staff would feel about it (they analyze *everything*), so I make sure to keep an eye on the clock to avoid room checks.

At 9:30 I pick myself off the floor and head down the hallway into the common area. I make my way over to Emerson and Zena lounging sleepily on one of the couches. Emerson stifles a yawn and nods in greeting. "G' morning. How much do you think I'd have to bug the nurses to get some coffee?" He closes his eyes and leans back into the cushion as Zena chuckles.

"You sound just like my dad. He won't go anywhere without his coffee. Brings it everywhere." She leans back against the arm rest and props her feet over Emerson's legs, linking her arms behind her head.

"What's the matter? You look like you're about to have family therapy," Emerson jokes, facing me. When I don't say anything, he raises his eyebrows. "Oh no, you *do* have family therapy!"

I nod. "Yea, at 11:00. Are they really that bad?" Since my parents are divorced, family therapy is separate.

Zena pipes up, "It all depends on who you have. I've got Webber, and he's awful." My mother's note said we'd be meeting with Dr. Webber. I tip my head back to the ceiling.

"What do you mean 'awful?'"

"Well, I guess he's really persistent, nosy, which means it's awful for us," she shakes her head, "You can't hide anything with him."

"Who do you have, Emerson?" A smile creeps across his face.

"Dr. Patin. She's a real softie in family therapy. Then again, my mom's a lawyer. I doubt she'd push too much with her." He closes his eyes again before continuing. "Try not to worry about it too much. It's probably going to be pretty awkward since it's the first one, but there isn't much you can do to change it." He shrugs sympathetically and holds back another yawn. "*Damn* I need some coffee."

At 11:00 I settle down in a round, leather chair and anxiously listen to the dial tone as the phone rings solemnly on Dr. Webber's desk. Webber is fair skinned, probably in his forties. To placate my anxiety, I take to looking around his office. On my right, there's a large window with shades drawn over it. Shelves line the wall behind his desk, filled of books with sleep-inducing titles and a few office supplies. A stapler, a bowl of push-pins, and some paperclips sit immediately behind him. Downright dangerous in the hands of a crazy. I mean, to think of all the things I could do with a *paperclip*.

"Hello?" My mom's voice crackles through the speaker, snapping my head back to the phone.

"Hi Marissa. It's Dr. Webber here with Willow."

I can practically hear the smile in her voice. "Hi Willow! I know it's only been a few days but I've missed you so much! How are you? How is everything there? Have you been sleeping ok?

You probably haven't had time yet, but don't forget about the journal! I read an article on journaling yesterday and it said—"

"*Mom*," I shout, bringing the anxious mom-train to a halt, "It's ok. Thanks for the journal, it was really nice. I've missed you a lot too!" I dodge her questions about how things are and ask instead, "is Dad there?"

Her voice is thick with caution when she replies. "Oh, Honey, I'm sorry. He called me this morning and said he wouldn't be able to join us. Conference." Even though my parents are divorced we were supposed to have this first session together to "lay some ground rules" for future therapy. Disappointment fills my chest.

It isn't that I wasn't exactly expecting this, but the sorrow in her voice hits me. Conferences are supposed to be scheduled ahead of time, right? He could have said *something*, and not the morning of. I can feel Dr. Webber's concerned stare on the side of my face and try to pull off nonchalance.

"Willow, how do you feel about that?"

I shrug and say loud enough to reach the speaker, "I don't really care. He has a conference. I get it." My skin prickles with budding annoyance.

"If you don't care, then what's going on with this anger?" The phone stays silent but for the faint sound of breathing.

His comment catches me off guard, and the frustration makes it hard to focus on lying. If he can spot that before I can barely register I'm upset, this is going to be a long session. "I'm just a little annoyed. He has a strong track record on being a dismal father." *Oh no! What did I just say?!* The prickling turns into a fire, and heat blooms up my neck.

How could I be so careless? I even said *father*, which is shrink for distancing language. My mom's voice echoes through the office, speaking before Dr. Webber can. "Oh, Honey. I'm so sorry. I didn't want to say anything, especially since he should have told you himself." She gives a weighty sigh, "I'm really sorry, baby."

A pause spreads out into the room. I scratch my nose, doing my best to smother these stupid emotions. Dr. Webber finally speaks. "Willow, I see this is a topic that's pretty upsetting for you." I don't confirm or deny it. "We can talk about it more on Monday in your individual session, but since we have your mom here, I'd like to focus on your relationship with her." I nod.

A sniffling sound comes though the phone, followed by a short series of coughs. I scoot forward on the chair. "Mom? Are you ok?" The phone stays silent for a few seconds before she responds.

"You're so sweet. I'm alright I—" she hiccups out a small sob and doesn't continue.

"Marissa, can you share with Willow what you're feeling right now?"

Another sigh makes the speaker crackle. "Well, baby, it's just *so good* hearing your voice. You have no idea." She blows her nose. "I know it's only been a few days, but the last time I really saw you was—". Again she stops. The heat creeps up to splotch pink across my cheeks and redden my ears.

The last time we really saw each other was in the hospital. After *that night*. Guilt worms its way through me. *No.* I refuse to think about that night. She *cannot* bring up that night. So, of course, Dr. Webber turns his eyes to me and raises his eyebrows, clearly waiting for me to elaborate. When I don't, he prompts, "Willow, can you give your mom a hand? What's going on?"

Resoluteness course through me. I stare at him with stone certainty. "Well, it can't be easy to send your kid away. I have support here, but my mom's all alone at home. It must be really difficult to carry all of it by herself." It's designer BS and earns a small frown from Webber, but surprisingly he doesn't push. I have a bad feeling he's reserving it for Monday.

With only a few minutes remaining, Webber has us exchanges

good-byes. He hangs up the phone before turning to face me. "Normally I like to take a few minutes to get your thoughts after a family session, but I'll cut you loose early today." He smiles. I swear, based on the amount of smiling per capita here, there has to be something in the water. I make mental note of it. "We can talk about it more Monday. The first week is always the longest."

I nod and say thanks. Standing up, I turn right as the door opens, revealing Anthony looking a little harried. Interesting. I got the vibe nothing rattled him. "Sorry for the intrusion. There's been a small situation in the common area, so I've come to walk Willow back." Double interesting. Webber nods and says thank-you to Anthony as we walk from the office.

I do my best to prod him for information, but he's tight-lipped. As we approach the common area, I listen for the sounds of shouting. We pass through it, quiet and without incident. Really quiet, in fact. I look up to Anthony. "Where is everyone?"

"They've all been sent to hang out in their rooms for a bit. Don't worry, we'll bring lunch up to everyone. Little known fact: Glenview has a five-star dining service run by yours truly."

Despite his light tone, the atmosphere feels thick. We get to my room and he gives me a salute and walks away. I close the door and sit on my bed, my mind still turning from the session.

Just thinking about the hospital makes that black thing inside of my stir. A shiver ripples over me. I can feel the memory trying to slither out and reel back the film. My fingers curl around the blanket, tightening into white fists as the black thing reaches a crescendo, crushing my ribcage and forcing air from my lungs. Tears well up in my eyes, like the kind that happen when you bang your shin against the coffee table. The kind that happen from an instant onslaught of pain. Against my pleas, a curtain of cold drapes over me, and now I'm pacing the room, trying desperately to outstrip my memories and the depression that follows.

Without a second thought I'm back on the floor. My breathing comes out strong and even with each sit-up. I do them until I can't count anymore. I do them until by abdomen is aching and quivering and it hurts to breathe. Next my arms are burning, a searing stronger than the emotional pain. I pump out a series of push-ups before starting on my triceps. The realization hits me with a gust of clarity; if I keep moving, I'll be ok. As long as my muscles are burning, the cold can't touch me.

A knock on my door tells me Anthony is back with lunch. I stand quickly and try to keep from panting while accepting a tray of unappealing hospital food. When he leaves, I set the tray on my desk but don't touch it. Not when this physical exhaustion wraps around me like a shield. I won't have time to eat any if I want to keep the black thing buried far, far down.

Putting an apple aside, I take the tray into the bathroom and empty most of the food into the toilet, leaving just a few bites to make the lie more palatable. My stomach grumbles in protest, and I make note to fill up on dinner. I flush the food away and walk out of the bathroom feeling just a bit lighter.

And as I exercise, I can feel the dementors recede. All the anxiety and shame and sadness wash away on rivers of sweat until a hollowness takes residence, a sweet undercurrent of apathy to float away on. When I finish the workout, I scarf the apple, eating right to the core. I gulp down a couple bottles of water to replace what I lost in sweat and thump gladly onto my bed, content to not move for the next week.

Chapter 4

When I plunk down into the same leather chair in Webber's office on Monday, it takes everything to keep down the flutters of anxiety. Quite a bit happened between Thursday and now. The "incident" no one was supposed to know anything about was circulated with shocking detail by dinner that night.

It was Piper. According to my sources, that is to say Zena, Piper had an epic meltdown. A category five catastrophe brimming with yelling and self-harm. No one is really sure the extent of her injuries; some versions happily report she had to get stitches, others say it was mere scratches and roll their eyes. Piper was taken to an ominous "quiet room" where the rumors get even more wild. Whatever the tale, she spent the weekend tailed by a staff member, waving her brightly wrapped arms for all to speculate on.

Across from me, Webber leans back in his seat and gives me a pensive stare. "So you and I will have individual sessions this time every Monday for an hour. What we talk about is, of course, up to you, but there are a couple topics we will need to discuss." His stare bores through me. I mean *come on*. It's been all of three minutes, and I already feel like he's caught me in a lie. Guilty conscience? "One of those topics being your recent suicide attempt." He pauses, gauging my reaction. The black thing rumbles. I can already feel my hands itching to bring relief. *Not here.*

Not yet.

"Like I told Dr. Wilson, there isn't anything to *discuss*. I've gone through it several times now, so I really don't see how detailing it again is relevant." Let the lies begin.

"He mentioned you seemed anxious to approach the subject, which is exactly why I would like you to talk about it."

"No." The authority in my tone surprises me. Webber's face doesn't change, but I pour all my energy into making my expression as neutral as possible. Unfortunately, in my time here I've learned masks only convey there's something behind them worth hiding.

"No? What do you think will happen if you share your suicide attempt with me?" That phrase again. Suicide attempt. Not "incident" or "accident". The directness cuts through my preplanned BS.

"Nothing. It's over."

"Is it really over for you? You're saying you don't think about at all? Don't have dreams or nightmares?" His words dig out a buried truth and before I can open my mouth to respond, something inside me breaks. In an instant, I'm engulfed.

Emotions rush through me like a ripping tide. Deep waves of anxiety crash over my head while shame anchors itself to my feet, pulling me down into the abyss. Depression waits for me at the bottom, arms outstretched in sinister welcome. My fingers reach covertly into my legs and dig in, the pain soothing the riptide into a swift current.

I don't know how long I can hold out.

"What are you feeling right now?" His voice drips with concern.

I don't say anything. If I open my mouth the water will rush in. I'll drown, trapped at the bottom of the ocean. Alone.

"Willow, I'm right here." His voice comes through muted and wet. "Focus on my voice. Breathe in, breathe out. Come on, Willow, you can do it. Breathe in. Breathe out."

But I can't breathe. There's water in my mouth. The pressure is compressing my lungs. I'm trying to swim but it's too far to the surface. It's too damn far.

"Focus on my voice, Willow. You're in my office. You're sitting in a chair. It's warm in here because the heat is on. You are safe." *Safe.*

Suddenly I can see the light above me, tantalizing close. Once second I'm clawing toward the surface, the next my lungs are drinking in the warm, oaky air in Webber's office. I look at him wide-eyed and shaking. He leads me through a couple more measured breaths before I find my voice. What the *heck* just happened? My face burns with humiliation. That was definitely not part of the plan.

"Sorry," I murmur.

"It's perfectly ok. You don't have anything to be sorry for. If the subject is too fresh right now, we can reserve it for later sessions. Ok?" I nod. "We have a few minutes left, and I'd like to ask a couple questions about your current safety. Is that alright?" Another nod. Looking down, I notice there's something sticky on a couple of my fingernails. I feel like a toddler who couldn't make it to the bathroom.

"Don't worry about the anxiety attack. I was going to ask these questions anyway." Anxiety attack? No way, my thing is depression. Then again *he's* not supposed to BS *me*. "Do you feel like harming yourself?"

"No." It strikes me that this is a lie.

When I look back at him his eyebrows are pulled together with worry, a ghost of a frown spotting his mouth. "Alright. When you came here we were extremely concerned about your safety. Last week you were suicidal, and today you say you don't have those urges?" I nod. "What changed?"

I'm tempted to reply with something snarky. *It was magic. Poof! Watch me disappear.* "I've met some other people here, and they all seem pretty hopeful. I guess it rubbed off." It's the best I can do, and Webber gives me another free pass.

He tells me I'm officially bumped to level one, meaning I can leave the unit for the cafeteria and gym. Stupid psych hospitals and their stupid level systems. Still, part of me feels lighter at the news. Samson has been going to the gym on campus every night, and I'm itching to stretch my room workouts into something more. I mumble a thanks and close the door.

I'm barely ten feet down the hallway when a shadow melts out from one of the empty offices and catches me by the elbow.

Piper.

I spin to face her and see she's alone. We both are. "Hi, Piper."

She grins. "Willow, right? Why are you here?" 'Here' being Glenview, not in this hallway or even in the existential sense, which would be preferable. I can't see a way this goes well.

"Depression. You?" I can be blunt right back.

"Willow has depression? You're a walking cliché." She waits for me to respond, but I don't bite. "I've got borderline personality disorder. Ever heard of it? Well if you haven't, it's a load of shit. Impulsivity and attachment issues and anger." She rolls her eyes. "Like I'm not 16."

I don't say anything. I would like nothing more than to run from this hallway, but I won't give her the satisfaction. "You said you cut just the once?" Her tone is excited.

"Yea. And?"

Before I can react she grabs my wrist and spins me. Piper holds my arm still and pushes the sleeve up, revealing hundreds of thick, cross-hatching lines. I try to pull free, but she tightens her grip. I'm about to shout a few four-letter words when I see her eyes. The fire in them is gone, replaced by something I can't name. Her voice comes out low, the bite gone. "Girl, you've got it bad. The other arm like this?" My silence is all the confirmation she needs. She lets go, and I shove the sleeve back down, storming from the hallway. Tears prick at my eyes, drawn in frustration.

This is the problem with lying. My lies are wound up tight like a ball of yarn with the truth hidden deep inside. All it takes is one snag to unravel everything.

And that was one hell of a snag.

Relishing my new level one status, I march myself down to the gym after dinner with Samson, Matt, Zena, and Anthony, a nurse, like I have for the past five days. I tried inviting Emerson along, but he gave a shy smile and said it wasn't for him. Piper hasn't cornered me since Monday, but I feel her eyes follow me around the common area, and she practically waves a sign whenever "unhealthy coping mechanisms" get brought up in group. She hasn't acted up, either.

I feel an elbow in my side and find Zena looking at me. "Are you good? You didn't have any dinner again."

"Oh, yea. Eating before a workout always makes me queasy."

"Yea I get that. Maybe they'll let you eat after. I'm already regretting that mystery spaghetti."

I smile and nod but the truth is, ever since Piper's meltdown, I've haven't been eating as much. The empty feeling in my stomach makes me feel more alive somehow. It chases away the emotions simmering under the surface that are powerful enough to swallow me whole. At home my wonderful father liked to complain that I moved too little and ate too much. I tried rationing out my food, but it never felt like it does now.

After an hour Zena practically drags me off the treadmill. She jokes that I'm training to run away from Glenview, and we trade increasingly outrageous scenarios until we split off to shower.

Unlike the hospital, the showers here are untimed and

supplied by endless hot water. The heat works soreness from my muscles while the steam soothes my lungs. I turn the dial until the water is a comfortable degree of boiling and wade under its warmth. I do this every time. Part of me feels like the scalding heat can chase away those cold depressive tendrils. That somehow I can trade lethargy for relaxation. It never works.

It's hard to tell if my depression is better or worse since coming here. Sure there are plenty of activities to keep me busy where given the chance, I'd spend my time under a pile of blankets in bed. But the amount of therapy here is unfathomable. Morning check-ins. Evening check-ins. Individual therapy. Family therapy. Art therapy. A smattering of groups ranging from DBT (Dangerously Boring Topics) to the dreaded shame resilience group. It's hard *not* to be depressed when you're asked several times a day to analyze your depression.

A funny feeling starts working its way up my toes. Like when your foot falls asleep, only ascending up my legs. My fingers start the same process until a wave of nausea knocks me into the wall. There's a cold trickling sensation on the back of my neck even though its seared by the water. I barely have time to panic before TV static fills my vision.

A dull pain radiates from my knees and forehead. When static starts to clear, I realize I'm on the freaking floor. I'm on the floor because I *passed out*. I bring my hand to my forehead, but it comes back blood-free. So do my knees. Quickly I rinse off and get out of the bathroom.

Immediately the fresh air clears up my vision, and the tingling ebbs away. I get dressed and spot a nice red lump shining proudly on my forehead. What just happened? I debate going to get a nurse, but something tells me to keep it quiet. After two bottles of water I finally feel ok again. My head is still throbbing and growing an ostrich egg, so I skip evening check-in. Recently I'd been using the time to *not* think about therapy, so one should ask questions if I'm not there.

I grab a book off my desk and tuck under the covers of my bed and try, with some difficulty, not to think about the shower incident. As I read about cheesy teenage romance, I keep hoping that by tomorrow the mark will be gone. The thought even follows me into sleep, spawning nightmares that chase away any dregs of relief unconsciousness may have brought.

Chapter 5

Tap, tap, tap. "Hello? Come on Sleeping Beauty. Time to get up."

"Mmmm. Too tired for breakfast." There's a girly, amused laugh from the doorway.

"That's what you said when I woke you up for breakfast, which was two hours ago. It's 10:00 and art therapy is in half an hour." I press my face into the pillow but wince at the pain in my forehead. A couple moments pass with Amanda waiting in the doorway and me resolutely buried in my sleep-cocoon before she flicks the lights on.

"Alright, alright. I'm getting up. Wouldn't dream of missing art therapy," I say with bitter sarcasm. The expectations these people associate with morning is astounding, especially since half the meds they dish out here cause drowsiness. Mine, of course, do nothing since I spit them out. It's the small acts of rebellion, I think, while still lying in bed, that make this place survivable.

"I'm not leaving until I see you get up." Her ability to reduce me to nothing more than a child only encourages me to stay in bed.

"Who's in there? Is that Willow? Em! Get in here!" A pillow zooms at my face and two bodies thump down excitedly on my bed. When I open my eyes Zena and Emerson are staring at me with an unadulterated amount of cheerfulness. Despite my efforts, a smile works its way through the pessimism until I'm grinning like an idiot. I grab the pillow and chuck it back at Emerson, but he dodges it and starts laughing.

"You have to wake up earlier than that to get me," he teases.

"What are you guys doing?"

"Well we couldn't let you miss *art therapy*," Zena responds with a look over her shoulder at Amanda, currently wearing an expression of utter disbelief at the amount of rule-breaking occurring under her nose.

"Both of you, off the bed! You know you're not supposed to be in each other's rooms." Emerson gives the mother-of-all eye rolls and runs a hand through his leprechaun hair before picking the pillow off the floor and tossing it back on the bed. He and Zena saunter out of the room, completely undeterred.

"Oh! I almost forgot, a package came for you this morning," Zena calls from the hallway.

"A package?" I give Amanda a look of mock-surprise. "Well why didn't you say anything?" To cement my point, I jump out of bed and walk to the door. PJ's are basically formal attire in a psychiatric hospital, especially on a Saturday. Five steps into my display of sass the static returns, and I have to slam a hand into the doorframe to keep from falling.

Amanda is at my side in an instant, putting her arm under mine and taking some of my weight. "Willow, hey, just take it easy."

"I'm fine, really. Please." The spots are starting to clear, but Amanda doesn't let go. She forces me to sit back on my bed and takes my pulse, putting the back of her free hand on my forehead.

"You are not fine. You have a high heart rate and clammy skin. Is this the first time you've felt this way?" She's in full nurse-mode, and all hints of her patronizing tone have evaporated.

"Honestly I'm fine. I just got up too fast." She shakes her head and stands up.

"We were going to wait until after group, but you need your vitals taken now. Are you ok to stand?" I nod and together we walk into the common area, Amanda glued to my side. Emerson looks up when we approach his couch and gives me a curious look. I smile and point my eyes to the ceiling, trying to convey that Amanda is just being annoying, but he frowns when I plunk down in the roll-y chair beside the nurse's station. Obediently, I hold out my arm as Amanda puts on the blood pressure cuff and attaches a pulse-ox device to my index finger. The cuff inflates, giving its usual uncomfortable squeeze before hissing out air. Amanda writes down the numbers but doesn't let me take off the cuff.

"We need to do one with you standing too." I glance back at Em, confused. He runs a finger across his forehead. When another set of numbers pop up on the screen, Amanda takes the device from my finger and waits as I peel off the cuff. Just when I think I'm free, she gestures to the chair. "Take a seat for a minute, Willow." Tiny pinpricks of fear make my cheeks flush conspicuously and my heart thrum even faster. I look up at Amanda, wearing a frown identical to Emerson's. "According to your vitals, your blood pressure is way down, low enough to cause fainting, and your heart is beating much faster to try and compensate. Do you know why that would be?"

"No, why would I? I'm not a nurse." How am I responsible? This isn't operator error.

"The two sets of vitals we just took are called orthostatic vitals. The numbers from yours indicate more than just mild dehydration. How much water have you been drinking?"

"Well I can't be dehydrated. I'm not even thirsty." Now

would be the perfect time to tell her about what happened in the shower yesterday, but the concern in her eyes scares me.

"It's possible to be dehydrated but not realize it. How much water have you been drinking?

"Um, I don't know. Like four, five tall glasses of water a day. I've always had that much."

She scribbles something down on my chart and flips up the top piece of paper. "It looks like you're scheduled to get blood work done next Friday, but I'll leave a note for Dr. Wilson to see if we can't move it up." Ok, this is definitely getting out of hand.

"Look, I just stood up too fast. Maybe I didn't drink enough water after working out yesterday or something, but I'm fine."

She leans against the desk, a picture of scrutiny. "Willow, it's ok. There's something else going on, and we're going to figure it out. Until we do I'm afraid you won't be able to go to the gym." I start to argue, but she shakes her head and ushers me over to a table full of craft supplies, ending the conversation.

This is *insane*, pun most definitely intended. It's been what, all of six days since I was awarded level one privileges? Now it's been revoked by the Queen of Overreaction. The only time I feel more ok, when the sadness takes a hiatus, is during those workouts. Without them I really don't see how I can make it. Those short reprieves were the only things between flushing my meds and stockpiling them. I can only hope my room exercises will be enough, because I can't live with depression's pain. I simply can't.

A drop of water splashes over the drying glue on my collage, wrinkling the strips of paper. I look up to see Amanda looming over me with two Styrofoam cups, undoubtedly filled to the brim with water. "Can I at least have my package?"

"You'll get it after you drink both of these." She sets them down and hustles off. Across from me, Emerson clips out an *E* from a magazine and doesn't look up when I try to catch his eye. I wave my hand animatedly, but he gets up and walks back down the boys' hallway. There's a soft opening and shutting sound, leaving me staring at his empty chair in shock. Did I offend him? What changed between now and when he was jumping on my bed?

He doesn't return to finish his half-baked collage, and it gets cleared away when group is over. On the other hand, the package turns out to be the greatest assortment of candy and diabetes-inducing food I've seen. Nutty chocolate and artificial cherry unfurl into the air. Lemon drops and caramels and sour straws swirl into the glorious conglomerate of confection that hits my nose. Gummy bears and starbursts poke through layers of sugary treats, and a laugh escapes me. I almost hyperventilate trying to inhale it all. I check the box and find that it's from my mom, of course. On the short list of people who know I'm here, only she would send a box exploding with so many different levels of gluttony.

Just my luck, it all gets swept away by a nurse, Naomi, into the nutrition room, as such things "are strictly reserved for snack times and movie nights". What I would *give* for a Hershey's bar. As they round us all up for the trek to the cafeteria, I spot Emerson standing next to the door. "Em! Hey!" He doesn't turn around and walks behind Naomi into the hallway. I push past Samson and Jeremy, tapping him on the shoulder. "Em, are you ok?"

"Yea, fine." He doesn't even turn his head. "What about you? What happened this morning?"

"Nothing. Amanda just freaked out and said I needed to drink more water. That was it. Are you sure you're ok?"

"Yea. Are you hungry for lunch? I'm starving." The detachment in his tone and the rapid change of subject makes me think he's hiding something, and I'm not privy to it.

"Yea, I guess." We get to the cafeteria, and I dish out

the least-mushy, refried-bean smelling food I can fine. So salad. I pocket an apple for later, defying the rule on snacking between meals.

Lunch does nothing to quiet the awkward tension lingering between Emerson and I, and I find myself counting down the minutes until group. Anxiety wriggles its way to my stomach, effectively filling me up before I can take a bite. I half-heartedly stab a tomato but move it around the plate. When Naomi tells us to wrap lunch, I shoot up and deposit my uneaten salad on a tray in the back. Turning around, I almost run right into Emerson. He's rooted to the spot, staring at me with his eyebrows raised and eyes wide. I want to ask him if he's ok again, but if he doesn't want to share, I won't bother him.

We walk back to the unit, the locks clicking audibly as we pour into the common area. Naomi pulls the door shut, trapping us back in. Not that I have anywhere to go, but the fact that I can't leave even if I wanted to (believe me, I do) still makes me feel uneasy. It's just another loss of the personal agency Glenview strips us of, which makes my small acts of rebellion quite savory. I speed-walk down the girl's hallway and tuck my apple under a pile of folded shirts and stride back to the common area before anyone notices I'm gone.

A bubble of excited squealing announces the arrival of five

therapy dogs, wagging gleefully into the room. "A little surprise for everyone today," calls Naomi. "Weekly Reflections has been canceled so everyone can spend some time with the dogs from Paws Therapy Service." A smiling golden retriever wiggles furiously over to me and plops right down on my toes. Jeremy and Zena join me in an hour of belly-rubs and butt scratches.

The handler, Jody, introduces us to 7-year-old Cooper, who is happily drooling on the hem of Zena's skirt. I run my fingers through the long, white fur on Cooper's belly, and he immediately closes his eyes with satisfaction.

Between the dogs and that empty high I'm riding, today is actually an ok day. Look at me, being positive. If someone shoved a DBT mood chart in my hand, I might even rate "happy" an eight or nine out of ten. I can't feel the slightest twinge of sadness or exhaustion, not a single wisp of dissociative apathy. I feel so good that a buzzing starts just under my skin, like I'm electrified. By the time we say good-bye to the dogs, I'm grinning as wide as Cooper.

Chapter 6

"We are *not* watching *The Lion King*. Way too sad."

"How about *Divergent?*"

"We watched that last week," I say.

"True. Harry Potter?" A silence of agreement works its way over us, and I squish farther down into the beanbag. "Harry Potter it is. I vote for the fourth one. Anyone second that?" A murmur of assent sets the wheels in motion, and behind me Jeremy starts humming the intro.

"Wait a minute." Naomi comes to lord over us, reminding me strikingly of Ms. Weasley. "Isn't that the one where that kid gets murdered?"

"Spoiler alert," calls Zena.

"Hold on. You're not about to tell us that it's 'too violent'? It's *Harry Potter!*" Samson's indignant shout raises more cries as we wait for the verdict. Naomi sets her hands on her hips, weighing the choice between the violent movie scene or a riot of teenagers. Outnumbered, she nods.

"Fine, fine. But don't get your snacks everywhere! You guys made a mess last weekend." Emerson whoops and fist-bumps Anthony sliding down on the floor to camp out with us. The excitement I felt earlier hasn't yet dissipated, and I happily indulge on my bags of sweets. I swap Zena a Twizzler for some Sweetarts and pop one in my mouth as the movie starts. As a secret Harry Potter geek, I must have seen the movie five times by now, but I can still feel my eyes widen with excitement. I mouth all of the lines embarrassingly committed to memory for the first half an hour until Zena takes a Starburst and throws it at my face.

It's hard to make out in the dim lighting, but I think it's either pink or red and pluck it in my mouth. I reach my hand reaches into the bag and scrape around for another. My pulse quickens when my fingers brush past only empty wrappers.

A lot of them.

I feel around in the Hershey's bag and the sour-punch straws container but find only granules of sugar. Did I eat *everything*? The darkness hides the telltale flush working its way up my face, and I can feel shameful tears well in my eyes. I know there are a couple of bags in the nutrition room I didn't grab, but the rest gurgles uncomfortably in my stomach. Apparently my cravings for sugar are insatiable, because now I'm frantically scanning the piles of wrappers for anything more. Despite how much I just ate, *I still want more.*

As a tribute to how panicked I am, I don't realize the

movie has ended until I get a knee in the back of the head from Jeremy as he stands. The lights flick on, and I scramble to wad up the bags, hide the evidence. Anthony unlocks the Nutrition room so everyone can return the snacks to their bins. I jam into the crowded room and do some quick thinking. In the same motion, I drop the wrappers in the trash and grab a Styrofoam cup from next to the juice machine. My bin is in the very bottom left corner and I slide it open, keeping my back to everyone as I furiously shove a handful of peppermints and M&M's into the cup and seal it swiftly with a lid.

I let myself move along with the crowd as people exit and drag themselves sleepily back to their rooms. I yawn wide, imitating them and do all I can to keep myself from running down the hallway.

"Night, Willow."

"G' night," I reply to Zena. The moment my feet cross the threshold, I close the door and press my back against it. Level One privileges bump my room checks from every fifteen minutes to every half-hour, but it still doesn't give me enough time. I stride over to the bed, pulling back the covers so I'm ready to jump under them at a moment's notice and grab the clock from the nightstand. The number changes to 10:01. Twenty-nine minutes, twenty-eight if I want to be safe.

With shaking hands, I pull off the plastic lid and tuck it in my drawer in place of the apple, which I remove. My feet pace a rut in the carpet while my fingers fumble with the mint rapper. I get it free and pop it in my mouth, hardly noticing the flavor as I immediately work on the next one.

In five minutes, I've decimated the entire cache. Even a hollowed out apple core sits on my desk, browning as it oxidizes. My feet still pace across the floor in frantic, utter panic, tracing a 'U' around the bed and back. Webber would call it anxiety, but this is so much more than anxiety. This is a smothering, humiliating shame. It's flapping my hands while the horror of what happened plays incessantly in my mind. It's anxiety that breaks the fucking scale, superseding anything I can describe.

The terror is inside me, ripping my stomach to shreds and clawing at my throat, begging to get *outoutout*. I wrap my arms around myself and boil over in trepidation as thick, fat tears race down my cheeks. On and on I pace, personifying the image of insanity.

At 10:20 I slam myself onto the floor, doing the only thing I know can reverse this. I try not to count the sit-ups, but my brain is on auto-pilot, pressing me to do one more, one more. Just one more and the panic will subside. One more and that ever-pressing memory will shut itself away. One—grunt—more and the world will right itself.

It doesn't work.

I don't care about the candy anymore. The only thing that matters is this *feeling*, this raw burning setting fire to my panic, forcing my thoughts onto nothing else. It's a sweet, beautiful relief from the constant cycle of "what if's" and self-deprecation, but underneath I know I'm just delaying the inevitable. At 10:27 I pick myself off the floor to get rid of anything incriminating. With my back burning, I walk to the bathroom and pull up my shirt. Sure enough, the carpet worked away a layer, leaving a lie of angry, stinging skin on my spine.

The wrappers go in the cup, and I shove some toilet paper over the top for good measure. Afraid that they'll find the apple core in the trash and bust me for having food in my room, I try to flush it, but the apple just spins at the bottom. 10:29. Water rises ominously. I take a deep breath, reaching down, and free the core. Without thought, I chuck it in the trash, put some TP over the top, wipe off my arm, and pull the covers over my shoulder as the door clicks open, pauses, then clicks shut.

I set the bed back up and walk to the center of the room. I realize now that the buzzing I felt earlier was never buzzing but a deep, impenetrable itch. Several times I slip back into bed, praying for sleep, wanting the exhaustion to carry me into a sea of unconsciousness, but it never comes. I slow down my pace dramatically, merely hoping to tire enough to fall asleep.

Finally, the door clicks open. I wait for it to close but instead a voice enters the room. "Good morning, Willow. Time to get up for breakfast."

Chapter 7

I swivel solemnly in the roll-y chair while a faceless nurse takes my vitals. This morning when I finally forced myself out of bed, I didn't need to look in the mirror to know my face is drawn and gaunt, my eyes rimmed by discolored skin. My muscles groan and ache with every step, like small grains of sand slide between the fibers. Every part of my body is stiff with lethargy, but my emotions are bankrupt at last.

I feel a mix between a car accident and a hangover. Right after I was diagnosed, I read everything I could on depression. I knew about the sadness, the emptiness and lack of energy. Increased and decreased appetite were things I only read about amongst a long list of symptoms, not experienced first-hand. Why did it happen, then? Why, when I'm doing everything I can to remedy this depression, did it rear its head in an entirely different direction last night? The only consolation being that today is Sunday, so I'll have some time to recover.

"Alright, you're all set. Much better than yesterday's, but keep on drinking water," Nameless Nurse informs me. At these words something inside me cringes, something else that's taken residence in my fractured psyche.

Sundays, besides therapy-recoup days, are notoriously boring. I walk over to the craft table where Hazel and Piper sit making bracelets with tiny rubber bands. In the middle of the table is a bowl with several different bunches of colored string and one rounded pair of safety scissors. Over the next two hours, I tie endless knots into a chevron pattern until the bracelet is long enough to wrap around my wrist twice. At the end I bring each string together and tie one large knot before cutting the excess.

I get up and walk over to an empty couch, entertaining boredom. The seconds stretch into minutes until a blissful wave of drowsiness breezes through me. Quiet enchants the atmosphere, measuring my breaths into something smooth and even.

"Yes, I think that is a wonderful idea. Go right ahead." Nameless Nurse is speaking to someone, but the sound washes over my mountain of melatonin. Darkness blankets my vision.

From somewhere behind me, low, uncertain piano notes break into the stillness. The pianist gains confidence and starts slow, playing a few deep notes punctuated by a high chord. More notes are added to the fray, pushing higher and higher into almost shrill tones, both terrible and beautiful. I sit up and watch Samson's fingers whizzing across keys as the melody builds momentum. His head nods in synch with every deep, thundering note and vibrant minor key.

The music comes straight from within him. He strikes the chords with ardent passion, filling the air with wanting and fear and agony. The reel pulses with things unsaid: calamity and disorder, madness and pain. His eyes are closed, lost in the rhythm. This isn't a piece he's memorized, and he doesn't have any sheet music in front of him. This is Samson. Not angry, or crazy, or lost. He rocks as it pours from him, weaving jarring measures into a tune that spins high into the air, breaking with complex dissonance.

The music starts to slow until one long, low note echoes throughout the common area. Samson rests his hands in his lap and just sits there, like he doesn't quite know what happened. A moment passes before the stun wears off, then applause erupts from every direction. I look around the room at the patients, nurses, techs, and even Amelia the cleaning lady clapping avidly. Emerson whistles and gives Samson a high-five.

Samson has created something more than music. For a moment we are all just people, brought together by our humanness. Not inferior and superior, not patients and nurses, simply people enthralled by one boy's talent and daring. A picture is worth a thousand words, but that *music* was so much more than music. It was a story, his story, and damn if he didn't do it justice.

The truth he displayed hits me harder than anything. To be that bare, that true and unfiltered is a completely different type of honesty. As I watch the people in the room exchange compliments and smiles and thanks, it sinks in very certainly how beautiful truth can be.

Immediately sadness storms in, my personal killjoy. That will never by my truth. It can't, not by any hopeful thought, be my truth. There's a rule, I think, about secrets, that they all die in the end. They either die from you, or with you. And as my secret will never make its way past my lips, I know which will become me.

Lunch and dinner pass with everyone still raving on our little concert. Samson seems neutral about the attention, not relishing it but not shying away, either. He reluctantly tells us how his mom forced him into piano lessons when he was young, but last year he finally got the nerve to quit.

"But you're so good! You shouldn't be allowed to quit, not with that kind of talent. Is that what happened with soccer too? You got too good and quit?" I expect rage to fill Samson, but his eyes reflect grief.

"Matt, shut the hell up, will you?" Matt drops the subject, and Samson stays quiet as we file back in to unit. I still haven't slept and stifle a yawn, battling a wave of tiredness from the perfume of steaming soups and hot chile. Winter's cold seeps in through the wall of windows, but the common area is the perfect degree of warmth to double my drowsiness. If I walked off to take a nap, or more likely a small coma, the nurses would chart it as a sign of worsening depression, so instead I find the least comfortable chair and tuck into it.

Nameless Nurse stands in front of us and starts gesturing excitedly. "Well everybody, I was thinking—"

"That's a problem," Zena mutters.

"—that instead of watching a movie tonight, we could play a game, everyone together." Zena's face morphs into the epitome of teenage exasperation and I bury a laugh. Nameless Nurse, who I'm just going to christen Jody, scans us for signs of excitement and plows right on as though she found some. "Has anyone heard of Bus Stop?"

"Oh, no. You don't mean that improv game?" Emerson's face is tragic.

"That's the one! Emerson, why don't you explain how it works?"

"I don't remember it too well, but basically there's two people at a bus stop, and one has to make the other so uncomfortable that they leave." Oh God, no. I never took a theater class since I like avoiding public humiliation, you know, when I can.

"Spot on. Alright, who wants to go first?" Matt and Piper pull up a couple of chairs next to Jody and turn them to face us. "Whenever you're ready."

"Hello there," Piper whispers.

"Uh, hi." Matt mimes reading a newspaper. Piper scoots her chair closer to Matt's until only an inch separates them. "Something I can do for you?"

"Oh, no," Piper croaks dramatically, "I just came back from Africa, you see. It was horrible, the guy on the plane next to me just kept coughing and coughing." She inhales deeply and starts hacking all around Matt. "I saw on the news today he died of Ebola. What are the odds?" Matt visibly pales and leans away from Piper, using his newspaper like a shield. "Oh it's *dreadfully* cold out here, isn't it? Do—do you mind?" Without another word she drapes an arm over Matt's shoulder and pulls him close.

"You know what, I think this is my bus. Yup, whaddya know. Nice meeting you!" He hops off the chair and bows as we all clap. "Thank you, thank you. What happens now?"

Jody chimes in, "Now Piper, take Matt's seat, and someone else can fill in where Piper was." Apparently feeling bold,

Emerson steps up to the challenge. He stands in front of the chair, composes himself, and dives right in.

"Hello there. Waiting for the bus?"

"Well, yeah."

"Me too, me too. Where are you from?" He leans back in the chair casually, but checks over his shoulder every couple seconds.

"Oh, just a few miles over in Bridgeport. How about yourself?"

"Sunny Meadows."

"Sunny Meadows?"

"Yeah, you know, the psychiatric hospital? I've just escap—I mean, left." I look over to Zena to see tears in her eyes, sputtering with restrained laughter.

"Oh, well, that's…well…" Piper clutches an invisible bag to her chest.

Emerson cast another nervous glance behind him and crouches down on the floor. "Listen, I'm not here, ok?"

"Ok. Um, w-w-why were you there? At the—place."

"Oh, a little of this, a little of that." His face turns serious. "But he had it coming. You *do not* insult the Seahawks without getting what's coming."

"You are totally right. You—" Piper's face turns red with

the effort to hold back laughter. "Ah, this is me. Good luck with…well good luck." She leans in close to the invisible bus driver and whisper-shouts, "Drive, drive, drive!"

Everyone is howling with laughter, bent double and gasping for air. Jeremy goes next, and Matt comes back for another round after him. By the end of the night, everyone's face, patients and staff alike, are painted with smiles.

Someone comes up behind me and pokes me in the ribs. "If you keep doing that, your face will get stuck." It's Emerson. "I don't think I've seen you smile so much."

"Well, that was fun! I didn't think people would get so into it. Pretty cool day, all in all." He nods and heads for the boy's hallway, but I stop him. "Hey, Em. We're ok, right?"

He turns around, looking a little guilty. "We're good. Talk to you tomorrow?" I nod in reply, and we part ways down the hallways. It takes less than a minute after my head hits the pillow to fall deeply, soundly asleep.

Chapter 8

Monday proves to be a quadruple threat: Amanda is on shift, I have individual with Webber, today's group is Psychotherapy, and, as promised, I'm getting blood drawn earlier than was originally scheduled.

In an effort to hold onto the last dregs of goodness of the morning, I wait until three minutes before group to drag myself out of my room and plunk down in my usual red armchair. Emerson inclines his head when I enter but doesn't say anything. Everyone is quiet under the normal anxiety psychotherapy group brings.

Dr. Patin walks in brightly and takes the empty seat at the front. "Good morning everyone! How were your weekends? I heard a couple of interesting highlights from staff this morning." Per usual she smiles from ear to ear, leaning forward and bringing her hands together in a show of eager interest.

"Well, Samson pretty much stole the show. Who knew we had a concert pianist in our midst?" Emerson is happy at the opportunity to direct the spotlight away from himself and looks expectantly at Samson.

"Yea, you were like, super good," Hazel quips. This gets

several head nods, and the interrogation officially begins.

"Samson, can you tell us about it? What did you feel when you were playing?"

He shifts uncomfortably in the squashy seat. "I don't know. It was weird; I haven't played in so long. It was different than how I remember it."

"Different how?"

"Well, before, it was so ridged. I played the songs I was told to play, and for hours a day. This felt different. It felt more…" He looks up at the encouraging posters, struggling to find the right word.

Zena supplies, "More natural? It was incredible. You made it look so fluid, like really honest."

"I like that, Zena. Honest." Dr. Patin shifts to look at us all, and I have a bad feeling about what's coming. "Why do you all think honesty is important? Is honesty important?"

Piper leaps at this. "I think it's important. I mean, how are we supposed to get better by keeping secrets?" With a surge of horror, she looks right at me. "Especially from friends. You can't build relationships with anyone if it's based on lies." An awkward pause expands into the space with Piper still staring right at me. I can feel my muscles knot up with dread.

Dr. Patin, in a show of incredible annoyance, doesn't miss

Piper's meaning and redirects the conversation. "Yes, I agree that honesty is a crucial component in treatment, both with doctors and ourselves. Piper, is there something you would like to say to Willow?"

"I'm not the one with something to say," Piper presses. "Why don't you ask her?" She is *not* doing this. Not now, not on this crappy Monday, not when my brain spins with fatigue and hunger.

I steel myself and stomp down the rising anxiety. "Ask me what, exactly? It sounds a lot more like an accusation from where I'm sitting. Last time I checked, I wasn't on trial."

Piper is on the edge of her seat, looking hungry. "Well if you won't tell them, I will." She lets the tension stretch on, building the stage. "Let's see, where to start? Maybe how you use your arms like a pencil sharpener? Or how you literally have too many scars to count, and you told us this bullshit on how you only cut once? I don't think you've had an honest moment since you got here." She's panting now, grinning madly with unconfined satisfaction.

What happened to the concern in her eyes when she forced my sleeve up? How did that person become *this*? I'm dully aware that I'm shaking, my chest rising and falling rapidly. My palms are flat against my legs, secretly tracing the armory of scars she has no idea about.

"Shut up, Piper! No wonder she didn't say anything about it. The only thing insane is how someone as horrible as you could be allowed to stay here." Zena is spits the words at Piper with as much girlish venom as she can muster.

"Let's all take a breath," Dr. Patin intervenes, supremely calm and unperturbed by the rising tension. "Zena, I can see you are angry, but harmful words never resolve conflict. And Piper, I know you are fully aware that no one is *ever* forced to share anything that they don't want to. It is Willow's right to tell us whatever she feels comfortable with. I want to speak to both of you after group." The damage is already done. Piper doesn't look the least bit affronted by Dr. Patin, and Zena is still fuming.

I look over to Emerson, staring at me with a mixture of shock and awe, his eyes wide with sadness. He just keeps staring, unbelieving, waiting for something. I can't tear my eyes away. "Willow? What are you feeling right now?" Dr. Patin's voice is soft and measured. I want to answer, I want to somehow find an antidote for Piper's words, but what can I say?

"I don't know. I don't…" Something breaks through the shock, through the sadness, something that feels strong and burning. Fuel with direction. "What can I say? I'm sorry Piper saw? That I should have done something when she cornered me in a hallway and kept me from leaving? No. She was looking for ammo, and she found it." I take a deep breath. "I didn't say anything because it doesn't concern anyone. It's about something I went through—am still going through, not a display for other people."

The words settle in the room, slicing through webs of tension. When I look back at Dr. Patin, I expect to see a frown, but she's smiling wide. I turn my head to Zena whose eyes bore into Piper's with a look of furious pride. Emerson studies the carpet, fidgeting with his hands absentmindedly but doesn't meet my gaze.

Something is off.

"Well said! I think we can all respect your decision to keep it to yourself. Thank you for trusting us and being vulnerable. It's not an easy thing to do." I nod in reply. The clock on the wall says that group ended five minutes ago. Dr. Patin dismisses us, minus Zena and Piper, with the recommendation to talk to staff if we should feel upset about anything from group, or anything at all.

When we congregate in the common area. Samson comes up and fist-bumps me, trailing a few colorful words after Piper's name. Matt and Jeremy also say they're on my side, and Hazel drifts to her room without a word. Only Emerson stays absorbed in his thoughts, keeping his back to me as he selects a moldy couch to plunk down on. I say thanks to the guys and cautiously head to Emerson. "You ok, Em?" His eyes are closed, and he gives no suggestion that he heard me. "I thought we were going to talk today?"

"Later." He still doesn't open his eyes. No goofy grin, no wrinkled nose, no mischievous head-tilt. Nothing about this boy is the Emerson I know. The group room opens and Zena and Piper shuffle out, the former unaffected, the latter distinctly disgruntled. I catch up with Zena and steer her away when Dr. Patin strides over to the nurse's station.

"Hey, are you alright? What did she say?"

"Not much, she mostly was mad at Piper. And when I say mad, I mean more patronizing than normal." She looks me squarely in the eye and sweeps away a stand of blond hair from her face. "What she did was not ok. It's Piper's twisted version of jealousy, and it's just another one of the messed up things she's done since coming here. Did she tell you she has borderline personality disorder?"

"Yeah, she did. I was wondering about that."

"Well I don't know if I buy it. People aren't even supposed to be diagnosed with personality disorders until after they turn 18." I give her an impressed look and she shrugs. "I'm thinking of majoring in Psychology in college."

"Thanks, by the way. For what you said in group. You're not like, mad? That I didn't tell you?"

She shakes her head. "Of course not. We all have our secrets here. No one is mad at you, except maybe Piper for showing her up in front of everyone." *We all have our secrets.* I wonder what she's hiding. I'm relieved to hear she isn't mad, but when I think of Emerson, I know that's not the same case. To add another layer of awfulness, Amanda approaches us carrying a small, plastic container.

"Hey, Willow! Sorry, we need to do the blood draw now. I promise to make it as quick and painless as possible." I incline my head to Zena and follow Amanda into a small room just off the nurse's station. Inside is everything you'd expect to see in an exam room: a grey table covered in white paper, a box of gloves, a biohazard container, and an assortment of other medical supplies. She has me sit on the table and roll up my sleeve.

I finger the cuff but hesitate. In my limited exposure, people tend to react badly to seeing my scars for the first time, judging them as me. The nurses in the hospital were undoubtedly the worst, shaking their heads and whispering just loud enough so that I could hear. Amanda sets the container on the table beside me and gives me a knowing look.

"I'm not going to judge you, I promise. Not only have I seen it all, but I've also been there." She slides off her jacket to reveal four, maybe five white, faded lines on the outside of her forearm. "Take your time, ok? There's no rush." Her compassion and vulnerability catch me off guard. Amanda, Ms. Overbearing, Ms. Smothering, a self-harmer? Has everything she said to me come from experience?

I push up the sleeve past my elbow. Hundreds of angry pink and purple lines are painted on my arms, shiny and lumpy and completely exposed. Amanda says nothing. She doesn't stare, she doesn't react. She doesn't treat me any differently. Instead she attaches a rubber tourniquet and taps the crook of my arm a few times, teasing out the vein. "Go ahead and make a fist." I oblige and she wipes off the skin with an alcohol pad. The smell takes me back, with nauseating clarity, to the hospital. The needle stings as it goes it. Out of the corner of my eye, I watch my blood spill into a vial. "You're doing great. Let me know if you start not feeling well."

Vial after vial fills up until there's a rainbow of brightly capped tubes laying in the plastic bin. "Alright, that was the last one. We're done. Do you need to lay down for a moment?" I shake my head and start toward the door, pausing when I reach for the handle.

"Thanks." It's all that comes out, and doesn't nearly cover my gratitude for her acceptance, but she gets the gist.

"No problem. And Willow?" I turn to face her. "If you ever need to talk, I'm here, ok?" I manage a small smile and a nod, leaving her in the exam room.

I'm in Webber's office, bracing for the discomfort and psychological dissection about to take place. He sets a pad of paper and a pen on his desk, ready to record the many facets of how necrotic my psyche is. "How was your weekend?"

My weekend? The one with the candy fiasco and sleep deprivation, or the one with magic music and bonding games? "It was fine. How was yours?" It feels awkward, these conversations, how he can ask things like "how are you" and "how was your weekend" without the obligatory reciprocity. I like to keep this catechism as level as possible.

"I had a good weekend, though it was colder than I anticipated. It's perfect bonfire weather, and I was able to take advantage of it. Can you elaborate a little more on 'fine'?"

"It was fine. Typical weekend." In a psychiatric hospital. He's doing the classic let-the-silence-stretch approach, and I bite. Much better on this than something more onerous. "We watched a movie. Played some games. It wasn't too exciting, and it wasn't too boring." Webber rolls the pen between his forefinger and thumb, clearly on the verge of getting to the real topic. Oh, joy.

"As promised, these sessions are here for you to talk about whatever you would like. Is there anything you have in mind for today?" The pen goes back on the paper, and he stares at me with the same disconcerting examination. There must be a class in shrink school on that mind-reading look. I fold my hands in my lap, meeting his gaze.

"Not really, no." Once again, silence etches away at the seconds, but I'm determined not to break it. Can that *please* be it? A weekend update and I'm free to go?

"Not really, or no?"

"There's nothing I would like to talk about." He relaxes into the chair.

"In that case, I'd like to talk about your family. Does that work?" Would he even drop the subject if it didn't? Still, the choice surprises me.

"You're not going to ask about group?"

He smiles. "Do you want to talk about group?"

"Not in the slightest." This earns a chuckle from Webber.

"So that brings us back to family. Let's start with your relationship with your dad. Tell me about him." I watch his hand edge slyly to the pen, moving under the impression that this is a topic worth writing down.

I take a small breath, exhaling newborn flutters of anxiety. "Um, he's an engineer. Very much a science brain. Likes hiking, long walks on the beach." I feel like I'm setting him up an online dating profile. *Enjoys reading Sara Dessen novels and cuddling by the fire.*

"That was a very diplomatic response. How do *you* view him? Last week's family therapy with your dad seemed like it made you pretty uncomfortable." This careful prodding is getting really old, complete with the body language showing only curiosity. And the thing is, I think Webber really does care. His interest seems genuine. But what's the point? Does he really think if I whine about my dad enough, they'll ship me home, good as new? He can't honestly have any expectations that I'll get better, because that would be naivety on a different level.

"I hadn't seen him in a while, of course there were some cobwebs to clear away."

"When was the last time you saw him?"

Webber and his uncanny knack to pick out the doomsday topic. My breathing quickens. I whisper, "Hospital."

"What about before then? Can you remember the time before that when you were with him?" He skirts right on by, and I feel a surge of gratitude. My bodily functions slowly return to stasis.

"Um, I guess it's been a while. Probably like three months."

This gets the pen moving. He scratches something down before looking back up at me. "Why was it so long? Is that normal for both of you?"

I sigh, slipping out a burst of frustration that has nothing to do with Webber. "It depends. That was one of the longer stretches, but even when I'm at his house, he's not really there."

His eyebrows pull together and tip up, a cross between concern and a frown. "When you say 'he's not really there', what do you mean?"

"Like half the time he's not physically in the house, working or going on long bike rides. But when he is…he's absent. I interact more with my dog."

"So he's not very present with you?" I nod. "How does that make you feel?"

"It doesn't make me feel anything. Look, it's fine. I get it. He's busy, or whatever. I really don't need him."

Webber actually smiles at this. "You don't need your dad? I don't buy it. I think you're more upset about his distance than you're letting on."

The frustration doubles, a generous portion now courtesy of Webber. "I don't really expect him to change, so there's really no point dwelling on it. I don't need him." Webber doesn't say anything but keeps smiling, like *I'm* being naïve. The frustration rises, it's surface tension taunt to break. "Yeah. It sucks. It has sucked. It will continue to suck. Nothing is going to change, so I really don't see the point in talking about it."

He studies me for a minute, the smile evaporating. "So you don't expect your relationship with your father to get any better in the future? That's a pretty hopeless thought." I look away, reading the spines of books behind his desk. He's waiting for me to counter, but I just shrug. Doesn't he get that it's not hopeless, the perspective, but hopeless, the fact? That my pathetic relationship with my father is just the model city version of the hopeless *reality* I'm facing?

The thought acts as a trigger, inviting in the freezing, energy-sucking depressive feelers that have been waiting since this morning. The cold trickles down my body until I'm effectively numb. The slurry fills up my lungs, and I can feel my body shut down, like someone flipped a switch. Or popped the thin, protective bubble my hunger affords. Out of the corner of my eye, I see Webber watching me, but I don't care. I don't freaking care about anything but what I know is waiting for me in my room.

"We're out of time, but for next week I'd like you to do a little homework. I want you to write a letter to your past-self. You can write to yourself at any age, and I want you to give your past-self advice. The advice can be regarding anything. Does that sound doable?" I nod, but the muscles in my neck already feel stiff. My knees pop as I stand to leave, and I trudge through the molasses and out the door.

Chapter 9

The new surge of exhaustion makes it difficult to exercise, but what did they say in DBT? Something about opposite action? So here I am, feeling a few minutes and a comfy bed away from sleep, yet wearing my hands into the floor with each mountain-climber. Technically everyone is supposed to be at lunch, but I told one of the nurses I wasn't feeling well from the blood draw earlier, giving me 45 minutes to "rest".

I expected to feel stronger by now, at least just a little bit, but if anything the workouts are harder. I'm out of breath easier, and my muscles tremble after just a few minutes. Still, I push on, sweating out the depression. It's funny, because like an addict, I have to do more, increase the frequency to feel the same relief. Exercise isn't a bad drug of choice if there had to be one.

So far I've avoided snacks altogether, terrified *it* will happen again, in front of everyone. I feel better eating alone in general and keep a rotating apple against the plastic lid in my shirt drawer. It's not *all* unavoidable, but I try to find the least crowded table in the cafeteria when I can.

Sounds of chatter drift in under the door, and I thump

backward onto the bed. My mind reaches, with much annoyance, to the "homework" Webber gave me. A note to my past self? I think I saw that in a movie once. He can't be serious? *Dear past self, just a heads up, your life is about suck, at lot. Don't worry, there's nothing you can do about it.* For the first time since coming here, I feel really homesick.

Not that my life before Glenview was dazzling or even normal. Interests? Hobbies? Wiped out by depression. Friends? Nonexistent, thanks once again to our star player. I ran track for three years, but the memory is so distant I can barely feel what it was like. To be happy, surrounded by friends, setting new PR's, trimming splits. It's like I'm reading about my life from a book rather than remembering it in full color.

I never even dated. Like I said, far from dazzling. The only parts I can remember closely are the few months leading up to…it. The festivity of fall froze over into an overcast winter. I kept my head down at school, sitting in classes with a glazed look, my notebook empty.

Lunches were so horrible I dropped them altogether. People don't always realize that the one thing worse than being bullied or harassed is not existing at all. I skipped the humiliation of sitting alone at lunch and walked around the hallways, waiting for the bell to ring. Sometimes I sat by the window in the library, feeling like my internal silence was finally matched by the environment. My brother is a freshman in college, so I was alone at home too. Alone with my dad. So freaking alone.

Amanda was right; depression really does love isolation. I remember wandering around the house, soundless, invisible, a hollow carbon shell. I remember everything hurt.

It's an unfathomable kind of pain. I can hear my father's famous words, "just be happy!", like gee, thanks, never thought of trying that one. The thing is, his words are born of inexperience. Until someone feels that kind of pain—clawing at the carpet, eyes wide with agony, muscles ridged like they've been tased—they have no right to pass judgement.

Here's the kicker, the stupid part of the whole stupid situation; my life is awesome. Not like Matt's, who struggles financially. Not like Samson, who lost the sport he loved most. I felt like this before I quit track. My mom is convinced it was the catalyst, but it was nothing more than a casualty of something already in motion.

Sometimes I wish there was a reason, like *aha!* Mark it on your calendars everyone, the magical date where that horrible thing happened and ruined the poor girl, so wasted. Which is probably the cause of those fatherly comments, or why everyone was so shocked to get that midnight phone call. *We missed the signs.* It's BS better than I could spin. *Stop complaining so much/you're so lazy/you don't even try anymore/would you get over it already?* Signs glossed over as character flaws.

It's fine though, really. I didn't want anyone to notice anyway. So, what would I say to my past self? What could I possibly do to prepare for the storm to come?

Get it right.

The click of my door jolts me from my thoughts. Zena stands in the doorway, bursting with excitement. "What is it? You look like you're about to explode."

In her hands are two black, phone-looking objects. She waves them enthusiastically and hops into the room. "Walkie-talkies!" A mischievous grin spreads across my face.

This just got a lot more fun.

The crackle of the walkie-talkie makes me pause, mid push-up. "Willow! Get out here already! Amanda swapped shifts, and I swear, I'm about to blow my brains out." The speaker dies, and I stand up, catching my breath. "You know, metaphorically speaking. Shit, I feel like I shouted 'bomb' in an airport."

"Swear to God, if you say that again I will *kill myself*.

Be right out." I rush to the bathroom and splash some cold water on my cheeks, but the pink doesn't wash away. On my bed is my brother's UNC hoodie, minus the strings, and I throw it on, disregarding the loose fit.

When I enter the common area I see Zena lounging on our favorite, least moldy couch. I thud down into the empty cushion and throw my feet across her legs, stretching against the armrest. "Happy Thursday! Did you get enough beauty rest?"

I laugh. "Plenty, thank you. Where's Em?"

She scans the room and shakes her head. "Sulking, his favorite pastime. Not a very happy camper this week, is he?"

I lower my head and frown. "Not at all." Emerson has continued his iceberg policy, spending as much time as he can in his room. He skipped shame group on Tuesday, and didn't come to any groups yesterday, gracing us with his presence only for mealtimes. When he emerged for dinner his face was drawn and waxy, his eyes rimmed with purple half-moons inspired by insomnia. Zena said he had a bad family therapy session last week, but I can feel that there's something more going on. Even when he walks it looks like it takes him enormous effort and barely any words press past his lips.

Zena and I have still been hanging out, ragging on groups and staying up late to chat with the walkie-talkies in our rebellious fashion, but our trio feels lopsided, wheedled down to two. Just my luck, Amanda approaches our couch, looking apologetic. "Sorry, Willow, but Dr. Wilson wants to see you." Dr. Wilson? Besides intake, I've seen him only one other time, and just to check how I was adjusting to the meds.

"But I'm supposed to have family therapy in ten minutes." She glances at the ground and taps her foot, betraying some negative emotion definitely not to my benefit.

"It's been rescheduled. Dr. Wilson would like you in your treatment team meeting." *What?* I can already feel subtle cues of panic flit in my chest and ricochet off my stomach. Treatment team meetings take place once a week and address each patient, but to my knowledge, no one is generally invited in. With much foreboding, I stand up and follow Amanda through the locked doors to a room I've never been in. She pushes the door open and gestures me inside.

It's a small room with beige walls, a rectangular table, and two couches and chairs occupied by three people. On one couch is Dr. Wilson, looking particularly scrutinizing and wizened. To his right is a new lady with a purple blouse and black pencil skirt. She must be younger even than Dr. Patin, but no less generous with smiles. In the last chair Webber sits with uncomfortably straight posture, looking serious and sporting a frown. Dr. Wilson addresses me. "Please, come in. I'm sorry to pull you from your activities, but there are a few things we would like to discuss." He must sniff out my ascending panic and adds, "You're not in any trouble, Willow. Please take a seat."

I sit on the edge of the cushion on the empty couch, rivaling even Webber's posture. It hits me with certain dread that nothing good can come of this meeting. Dr. Wilson mirrors the mystery lady's smile and takes point of the conversation. "How are you, Willow? Have you settled in ok?" *Settled in?* I've been here for 18 days, according to my mental calendar. Kids usually stay four to five weeks, which means my time for settling in has long come and gone, unless he means I'll be here longer?

"I'm fine. I'm sorry to be blunt, but why am I here?" Dr. Wilson's eyebrows shoot up in amusement.

"To put it simply, we are all concerned about your health. The nurse logs indicate that your blood pressure and heart rate have been consistently abnormal, and the results of your blood test drew our concern even more." His words hit me like a smack, sending heat slithering across my already flushed cheeks.

"Ok. I understand the need to be thorough, but I feel perfectly fine. One of the nurses mentioned I was a little dehydrated, and I've made the effort to drink more water since then."

Dr. Wilson leans forward, making his glasses slide a little down his nose. "Unfortunately, I don't think we're dealing with simple dehydration. Can you tell me about your diet?"

He can't be serious? But one look at Webber's face is all the confirmation I need. "Well, I eat the cafeteria food, so whatever they are serving."

I feel Dr. Wilson's piercing stare burn a hole in the side of my face, and I defiantly meet his eyes. "The worry here is that you may not be eating enough. Staff have noted you ritualistically skip breakfast and eat little at meals. This has an effect on you blood pressure, as we are seeing, and can't be fixed by drinking more water. Moreover, your lab results demonstrate the values of someone malnourished."

His words leave me dumbfounded, and my face burns like I've been struck. Maybe he's bluffing, trying to get me to confess to a crime I didn't commit. "I'm not malnourished, and I eat plenty a day. I'm not even underweight. And I don't eat breakfast because I actually like sleeping in, which is also important to my health."

Dr. Wilson opens a file and sets it on the coffee table. He shakes his head and traces a finger along flagged numbers.

"You are suffering from multiple nutritional deficiencies to the point of malnourishment. Your potassium is low, and your sodium and calcium levels are also in the abnormal ranges. These values and others correlate to a restrictive diet, and I want to be clear that it takes time to reach the numbers you have, longer than the two and a half weeks that you have been here."

My heart is thundering alongside the surges of adrenaline fueling my muscles, making me want to run. This must be a mistake; he *has* to be lying. But even as fear pulses swiftly through my veins, something inside me feels elated, *happy*. "You also have a high amount of ketones, from rapid fat breakdown, and phosphorus, which is a sign of muscle waste. We see this commonly in patients who compulsively exercise." He finishes reading from the file and closes it, looking up at me expectantly.

"I don't know why that would be. I mean I enjoy working out, but not to the point that its excessive or compulsive. Besides, I'm not allowed to go to the gym, which I should point out *is* excessive."

Dr. Wilson surveys me over the top of his glasses. "Is that so? You haven't been exercising at all?"

I shake my head. "No." The lie is so obvious he smiles, like the attempt was so feeble he found it entertaining.

"Starting now, you'll have orthostatic vitals taken three times a day. You will get weighed daily and work with Emily here to develop a meal plan, which staff will be monitoring. I know this sounds harsh, but if your blood work doesn't start to improve, then we will have to put you on room and bathroom restriction, which means you cannot go in either of those areas unaccompanied by staff." The words ring in the tiny room, bounce between the walls of my skull.

I plead, "I think you are taking this way too far. I'm sorry, but I don't agree with or see the benefit in any of that. Getting placed under a magnifying glass won't be, in the slightest bit, productive for anybody." I put as much conviction in my voice as I can muster, but I know it's a losing battle. Numbly I hear him supply a predictable, for-your-own-good response, but the sound is muted over the blood whooshing in my ears.

Emily introduces herself as a nutritionist, or dietitian, or whatever. We'll meet once a week, talk about food, etc. Only Webber remains silent, sending palpable waves of sympathy and worry through the room. Someone tells me I'll get a fifteen-minute phone call in lieu of family therapy, but the only words I hear are the ones telling me I can go.

Dr. Wilson walks with me to the door before unlocking it.

I step back into the unit, but he calls after me. "Oh, and Willow? Please take your medication, it's only there to help you." I walk away from him and listen as the door clicks shut. My feet automatically steer me toward my room, but what if they catch me exercising? Emotions are swirling through me with such ferocity that the edges of my vision blur out of focus. They need to get *outoutout*.

One way or another.

Amanda says something with the likes of condolences as I pass, but I keep walking. I pull open the door to my room and shut it quickly. My hands scrape around the drawer until my fingers brush against the flimsy plastic, and I pull it from the pile of shirts. *They can't do this. They can't do this. They can't do this.* I shut the bathroom door behind me and get crafty with the plastic lid. My hands shake while I work free the fabric on my sleeve. Cool focus settles over me as I begin to work, carving it all out, again and again, until my white shirt is no longer white.

I feel numb with relief. Apathetic. Hollow. The sound of the tap stirs my thoughts as I clean up, but they stay blissfully just beneath the surface. Somewhere in my room the walkie-talkie crackles to life, Zena asking what's going on, am I going to miss DBT group? I shut off the water and look in the mirror. My mouth twitches upward, just barely. The grim satisfaction in knowing nothing has changed.

Nothing will change.

Nothing.

Chapter 10

As much as I want to take Emerson's lead, I force myself to participate, smile, engage. They can't know how devastating these stupid rules are. And I wasn't lying about feeling fine. Dismiss the fatigue and muscle cramps and nausea, and I'm one of the healthiest people here. Still I go through the motions, spending time with everyone, commenting in groups, even changing my cafeteria routine, although I didn't have much say on that one.

A nurse sits beside me at every meal, at each snack, watching. Do they realize how incredibly unnerving that is? I push the food around but don't touch anything. The only semi-good aspect of all this is that I can't go crazy on snacks, not with eyes glued to the back of my head. I can feel the urge rising, coiling up like a snake.

I pray it remains entranced.

This lovely Friday morning, when I slept in, per usual, Anthony approached me with a "replacement shake", but who really knows what's in it? I grabbed a water from the nutrition room, fitted it with a lid and straw, and grabbed a spare lid for the shake since he poured it in the same container. What was he afraid of? That I'd chuck the plastic bottle at him? Or—God forbid—I actually *read* the nutritional label? Probably. Anyway, I drank the water, the shake's doppelganger, and tossed that chalky brown liquid in the bin, no questions asked.

    I've decided to take my phone call today and gladly flee for the privacy of my room. They gave me one of the basic phones awarded to level two graduates, so everyone but me and Piper. Dr. Wilson said 15 minutes, I'm tempted to stretch that a bit. I dial my mom's number and listen anxiously as it rings. She picks up on the second ring.

    "Willow? Is that you?"

    "Yeah, it is! Sorry about yesterday, but at least we can just talk now."

    She laughs, the phone editing it into robotic tones. "It's ok, it's ok! Dr. Webber called me yesterday, and explained—"

    "I don't want to talk about that. Please." The line goes quiet for a few seconds.

    "Ok, sorry. I'm just worried. I'm your mother, and I'm going to worry."

    "I know. It's really ok though. I mean there're nurses everywhere, so it's fine. But tell me about how things are there! How's Dante? I bet he loves the cold weather."

    "He does! As you know it's been cold here for a while now,

but he doesn't let snow stop him from dragging me on walks. You'd never know he's 13." Heat creeps up the back of my neck, something in her words igniting a thought just beyond my grasp. "But, more importantly, I have a surprise!"

"What is it? Don't leave me here!"

She laughs, this time a rich, joyful sound. "I hope you don't have plans for the weekend, because I'm flying down! Dr. Wilson and I spoke about it, and because of your labs, he didn't want you to leave, but I told him it's been *two and a half weeks* since I've seen my baby, and I'm coming down!" This time I'm laughing, actually laughing, and I roll on the bed, facing the ceiling with my feet in the air.

"Really? You're serious?! Way to tell him off, Mom! When do you get in? And what do you mean I can leave?" The heat creeps back down, placated for now.

"Yes, I *am* serious! My plane lands around 11 or so tonight, but oh, I forgot you're an hour behind. And you have a day pass for Saturday and Sunday. All day." Some light emotion in me soars, and my legs *fwump* back on the bed.

"This is insane. I can't believe it! Thank you, seriously." I look at the clock on my nightstand, noting that 25 minutes has elapsed. There's a knock on my door and Anthony leans against the frame. "Ok, well I have to go, but I'll see you tomorrow! We can do whatever you want."

"Alright. I love you, Honey!"

"Love you, safe flight!" The line disconnects, and I snap the phone shut, satisfyingly so, before handing it back to Anthony. Anthony pushes off the frame, and I walk past him into the common area, unable to feign happiness any longer.

When I finish relaying the news to Zena, she squeals in that pitch only best girlfriends can reach. "That is so exciting! I can't believe no one told you sooner, but *ohmygod* that's amazing. Wait till you tell Em." She mulls this over for all of three seconds. "Actually, don't tell him. He's *still* pouting." Zena rolls her eyes but behind the annoyance, I see a twinge of fear.

"I don't know. Don't you think it's strange?"

The fear becomes more pronounced, but she keeps all traces of it from her voice. "Nah. Em is a big boy, if he wanted to talk he would. Besides, he'd probably bite your head off if you cornered him."

"Yea, true." I try to push the thought away, but it hangs in the air, buzzing around. People bond fast here, seeing as we're expected to share intimately vulnerable details with complete strangers, so I can't totally dissolve my worry about Emerson. Something isn't right; I just wish I knew what it was.

The rest of the day goes according to schedule, which is pretty irksome. My arm gets squeezed six times a day, nurses hover close by, and after just a day and a half I already feel myself start to burn under the magnifying glass. To top it off, my small acts of rebellion have pretty much been cut to zero, so I keep the insurgency in my thoughts alone.

I would really love to say that despite everything, the newfound tyranny, the self-harm, the inability to exercise much, news of my mom coming just sweeps it all away. Goodbye smothering rules, goodbye depression. But it doesn't work like that, no matter how much I convince myself it does. It's more of a life preserver than a carnival ride, and I cling to it.

Somehow when they send us off nice and medicated for sleep (I still haven't given in), my eyes droop heavily and dreams sweep me away in mere minutes, scene after scene of hugging my mom. Scene after scene of a blurry boy with red hair, alone on a bridge.

Chapter 11

I'm already awake when Naomi clicks open my door at 7:30. An hour ago nerves threw me from sleep and I've been pacing the room, laying out clothes and putting them back, straightening the bed again and again. My bathroom mirror doesn't inspire confidence, but I braid my hair into a brown plait and try desperately to scrub away my sleep-deprivation rings. Not much success.

At 8:00 I resign myself to the least wrinkled sweatpants and my best hoodie, which may or may not be my only hoodie, nix the strings. I'm one of the first arrive in the common area. Matt has a sci-fi book and curls up in one of the armchairs, and Hazel rests comfortably the length of a couch. I consider making myself comfortable, but the excitement and nerves churn rapidly in my stomach, so I settle for pacing around the room.

The wall of windows displays a brown, dead landscape deep in winter's grasp. I rest my hand against the glass and feel the cold press into my palm. "Oh, Willow! Good, you're up. Come over and get your vitals." I saunter over and sit in the famous roll-y chair, sticking out my right arm and stifling a yawn. Naomi attaches the cuff and I wait as it inflates. "Did you sleep well?"

I shrug. "Yea, I guess." The cuff deflates and I stand for round two.

"No breakfast for you this morning?" She writes down the second set of vitals and sets the clipboard on the desk.

"No, I slept in."

Naomi nods and writes this in the chart. "Alright. I'll get you a shake." She disappears, behind the desk. I try to imitate her, but she's back in less than a minute.

"Thanks." Naomi hands over the mysterious brown liquid and resettles behind the nurse's station desk. I bring it to my lips but a voice rings out, *no!* The cup hovers in front of my mouth, not moving down but not moving closer. I lift it to my lips again, and again a voice screams out. *Stop! Don't do it!* I stare at the shake. The liquid forms a rim near the top of the Styrofoam, little bubbles gliding across the surface. I set the cup down. My stomach gurgles.

I wring my hands anxiously and take to pacing the room again. Piper stalks in on my second lap and claims a beanbag in the corner. She doesn't acknowledge me. I do the same.

After about 15 minutes, Naomi gets up and stops me. "What are you doing? Did you drink the shake?" She has her hands on her hips, and although we are the same height, she towers over me. Naomi looks at me with that special brand of maternal scrutiny.

"Sorry. No, I didn't drink it. I'm just not very hungry this morning."

Her eyebrows pull upward in concern and she crosses her arms. "Are you sure? If you don't drink it, I'll have to mark it in your chart. I know you are anxious, but your mom isn't arriving until 11:00. Is there something else going on?"

I shake my head. "Nope. Just not hungry." She walks away and pulls over a chair gesturing for me to sit opposite her. I oblige.

"Talk to me." Her eyes move to the shake. "What's going on?"

I'm caught between the desire to tell her, and my allegiance to keep lying. *What's happening?* "About the shake? I'm just really not hungry." I glance toward the boy's hallway, and the guilt expands into my empty stomach. Naomi follows my gaze.

"Alright, but there's something else on your mind. Maybe I can help."

Without moving my stare, I say, "Emerson. How's Emerson? Do you know what's going on?"

The silence pulls my eyes back to her. Naomi's face is all

sympathy, head tilt and frown to match. "I'm afraid I can't give out details about other patients, but Emerson isn't doing well. He would probably appreciate some friendly company right now." I look away again, out at the browning foliage beyond the window. Part of me waits for her to ask if I'm doing alright, but she doesn't, and I'm incredibly grateful.

When I still don't say anything, she pats my knee and collects the shake. I watch the wasted liquid slide into the trashcan and splash against the liner. Zena doesn't make an appearance until 10:30, and at the same time I'm whisked off to the exam room. Naomi hands me a gown and I hastily change into it, step backward onto the scale, and slip back into my sweats. 10:45. I take to pacing the room and shooting anxious glances down Emerson's hallway.

10:55.

Zena takes my hand and forces me into a chair. "Would you stop that? You're making *me* nervous." She plays with my braid as we wait. 11:00.

11:05.

"Do you think there was bad traffic? Maybe she got lost?"

"Willow, I love you, but you need to calm down. She'll be here at any minute." At 11:06 the sound of retracting locks snaps my head to the door. It swings open and in walks my mom, shoulder length brown hair pulled into a pony tail. She's wearing a tan, full length coat, jeans, and a black, floral shirt. Her eyes sweep the room all of two seconds before landing on me, and her face explodes into a smile.

I leap from the chair and run into her arms. "Oh, Willow!" Her voice is muffled by my shoulder. "It's so, *so* good to see you!" She hugs me suffocating tight and sniffs into my shoulder.

"Mom. Can't…breathe." She laughs, that wonderful, strong laugh and pulls me back at arm's length. Her eyes move up and down my body, looking for signs of distress or, more likely, new members of my secret army.

She sniffs again and pulls me in to a softer hug. She smells like honey-vanilla shampoo and makeup and home. To my relief, she doesn't say anything like, "you look sick!" or "honey, you're so thin". Instead she looks me in the eye, smiling radiantly. "Well, do you want to give me a tour, or should we get going?" Her happiness is infectious, and excitement hums in me.

"Let's get out of here." She laughs and Naomi buzzes us out. I look over my shoulder at Zena and wave.

She yells, "Have fun, girl!" I give a thumbs up and walk down the hallway. For the first time in 20 days, fresh air cascades over my skin. I drink it in, laughing gleefully into the bitter air.

We blast down the highway in a tiny rental car. My window is down, and freezing air streams into the car, making tears run down my face. I stick my hand out the window, sailing on currents of cold. I'm greedy for the fresh air, however freezing, but after five minutes my mom gives me a withering look.

"Alright, alright. You're no fun!" I have to shout over the wind.

My mom laughs. "I'm not trying to freeze to death here!" My eyes catch in the side mirror, reflecting the image of a girl clearly straight out of the nut house. My hair is wild, whipped loose from the wind, and my cheeks are bright pink. I tie the loose ends back.

"So, where are we going?"

"Wherever you want! Everything is east of here, but we can do anything. Go back to the hotel, watch a movie, go shopping. How are you doing on books?" In DBT group we are asked to describe how emotions manifest physically, like how fear makes your heart race or how embarrassment makes you blush, and I can say, with complete certainty, that freedom feels *light*. Feather-light, like nothing is tethering you down, like you are invulnerable. I fill up on it.

"I don't care." The concept of *choices,* of possibility makes me giddy. An idea pops into my mind. "I really loved the snacks you sent, but I shared some with the other kids. Could we stop by the grocery or Walgreens? Then we could go back to your hotel and catch up." The lie doesn't come out as effortless, but it comes out nonetheless.

"You got it." She steers the car through a valley, snowcapped mountains yawning high above us on either side. A streams works its way beside the road, the water bobbing over smooth stones and winding between a forest of pine trees. I rest my cheek against the window and soak in its cold, tilting my face to the cloudless sky.

The road winds into a city. Small mounds of grey snow melt on the shoulder and the car spits out slush as we roll by. My mom pulls into a gas station and hands me a twenty. I wrap my arms around myself and run inside, relaxing into the sweaty heat of the building. The candy isle doesn't disappoint, and I do all I can not to take one of everything. I pay the cashier and waddle back out, curling my hands into the cuffs of my sweatshirt.

I drop the bag of Sprees and Gummy Bears in the back seat and breathe into my fisted hands. My mom opens and shuts the door, bringing a gust of biting air. She sees me turtling in my hoodie and chuckles.

"Here, l-let's get the h-heat blasting." She turns a knob and cold air billows out from the vent. I cringe. "This might be the f-first place I've been where it's *colder* than it is at home!" We pull away and meander back through the city, weaving through towering office buildings and city-worn apartments. The air warms a few degrees.

"I mean, it sucks out here, but it's actually kind of pretty," I comment.

"It is beautiful. Ah, here we are." We pull into the hotel parking lot and sit in the car, not wanting to leave the heated interior. "Count to three?" I nod. We yank open the doors and sprint into the lobby, slipping on patches of ice and salt. The hotel is blissfully warm, and feeling works its way back to the tip of my nose.

My mom leads me up the elevator and into a small room. I set the bag of candy on her bed and look around. Despite having only been in town for 13 hours at most, her stuff is spread out all around the room: pillow and coat laid out on the bed, assorted beauty products strewn across the bathroom counter, and luggage dropped haphazardly in a corner beside the desk.

She sits in the desk chair and I take the bed. An awkward silence bubbles out into the room, and I shift around. The excitement of being out of Glenview and seeing her has made room for the anxiety of things unsaid. The way she folds and refolds her hands tells me she feels it too.

"Did you have a good flight?"

She perks up. "Oh, yes. It was fine. It snowed just west of us, and I was worried it might have been delayed, but thankfully our plane was on time. So tell me! How are you? What is it like? Have you made friends? When Dr. Wilson called me Thursday, I was so worried!" She looks me over and stops. "Sorry, I don't mean to bombard you. We have all day to chat." Dr. Wilson called her *two days ago?* Could all of that happened in the last 48 hours?

"No, it's alright! I get it. Well, I mean it's ok here. Not exactly what I had in mind for winter break." She smiles uncertainly, and I push on. "I have a few friends, yeah, but I mean we all sort of live together, so everyone knows everyone pretty well." I leave out any response about Dr. Wilson's new dictatorship and cross my legs on the bed.

"I know this isn't where you wanted to spend your break. It's not what I wanted for you either." Can it get any more awkward? "But I'm glad you're making friends. Dr. Webber said you've gotten close to a couple of the patients, and I'm so proud of you." The word "patients" hits my ears as a slap, and the fact that my mom is *proud* of her 16-year-old's ability to make friends sends heat waves of embarrassment into the room. "Honey, Dr. Wilson was really worried about your health. He said you hadn't been eating enough?"

She looks at me, smile-less, waiting for confirmation. "I don't know what he told you, but I've been eating plenty." To cement the point, I tear open the package of Gummy Bears and toss a couple in my mouth. My mom stands from the chair and joins me on the bed, walking like the floor is made of glass.

"Well, you *look* healthy. But he was adamant that you were undernourished. He even expressed the need to stay longer." I almost spit out the wad of Gummy Bears and spin to face her, fear dripping down every crevice of my face.

Swallowing, I respond, "Mom, that's crazy. Please, don't let them keep me there longer! I look fine because I *am* fine. Please believe me." She runs her hand down my arm and gives me a searching look.

"Ok. I'm sorry. I don't want to upset you. I just want you to be healthy and safe."

"It's ok." I nod toward the TV, desperate for a change of

subject. "Want to watch a movie?"

"Sure!" I know, it's lame. She flies halfway across the country to visit her daughter, who the last time she saw, tried to kill herself, and I insist we watch a movie. Something I would be doing anyway. But the thought of shopping, or going out to the movies, or going out for a meal, sounds exhausting. I lean back into the plethora of hotel pillows and settle in as we decide on *The Hunger Games*. With a smile of satisfaction, I think how the movie would definitely be vetoed at Glenview. I can almost picture Naomi strutting over, *"You are not watching a movie about homicidal teenagers!"*

My smile falls away. I *knew* this was coming. I could feel it just under my skin, like a sickness. That first handful of Gummy Bears sent fireworks exploding through my synapses. The sugar acts like a drug, and I can't get enough. I'm trying so hard to eat one at a time, savor the candy, but one turns to three turned to five, and now only empty bags litter the bed.

The familiar panic creeps into my throat, spiraling up my neck, perspiring my palms. The movie ended maybe twenty minutes ago, and my mom looks over at me. Worried. "Are you alright? You look a little flushed."

I smile and lean back against the pillows, praying she can't feel my heart beating furiously through the sheets. "Yea,

I'm good. I'm, uh, kind of tired. Do you mind if we stay in for lunch? You could grab something, but I'm pretty sleepy."

Her easy smile vanishes into one of frantic worry. "Are you sure you're ok? Should we go back?" She presses the back of her hand against my forehead.

"Mom, I'm really fine. I've been stuck inside the same four walls for the past three weeks. This is just a little draining. I'll just rest, and then I'll be good to go."

"Ok, but if you feel bad, at any point, please tell me."

I nod. "Deal." Seriously? She was about to take me back? After flying down here, spending money on a hotel room and rental car and who knows what else, she would send me back? "Isn't there a restaurant in the hotel? You could grab some lunch, and I'll take a quick nap."

I can see her weigh the options, mentally evaluating if leaving me alone is worth the risk. "Ok, but I won't be gone longer than 45 minutes. If you don't feel good, come down and get me. I can bring you something back up." 45 minutes. I can work with that.

"That sounds good. But you don't have to bring anything back. We have late breakfast on weekends." I'm a horrible person, lying to my mom, but any traces of guilt are worn away by overuse.

She grabs a room key and her purse, looking at the door then back at me. "45 minutes."

I stop myself from rolling my eyes. "I'll be here." The mechanical door thuds loudly behind her, and I leap from the bed. I look at the clock, adding the time 45 minutes from now, and search for the spare key. My eyes scan over the heap of pillows and piles of clothes, over the desk and the floor. I walk into the bathroom and sweep the counter top, finding the key under a clean towel.

To make sure she doesn't double back and change her mind, I count to 100 before lacing up my shoes and setting out the door. I walk quickly to the elevator and jam my finger into the down button, but it just dings solemnly. Impatience works its way into my muscles, and I jog down the hallway and shove open the door to the stairs.

It has to be on the first floor. They're always on the first floor, next to the pool. I fly down the stairs and push open a door marked with a red 1. People walk up and down the hallway from the lobby to the pool, and I slow down my breathing, mimicking their casual strides. I follow signs to the gym behind a couple of loud kids. Finally, I spot the door and slide the room key through the sensor. The light turns green, and I yank the door open.

The room is empty. Beautifully empty. I select a treadmill in the back and watch the miles per hour climb higher and higher. My feet hit the rubber, and I quicken my turnover to match the pace. *There*. Right there, that burning in my lungs. The searing in my calves. I sprint into nothingness, imagining the Gummy Bears obliterated in my stomach.

The room is lined with mirrors, and I can't help but catch a glimpse. My legs ripple with each step, and my arms look atrophied and flabby. I can hear my dad's voice come through the TV, telling me that I'm lazy, *how could you eat so much junk food?* For so long I've pictured myself, like a future, ideal self, looking like the other girls at school. The ones with *friends*, with perfect hair and flawless makeup. I picture their incredibly short shorts and skimpy shirts, and regardless how small their clothes were, the girls were always smaller.

Day after day after day after day of happiness measured by the space between you and your clothes, showing off thigh gaps like crowns, collar bones like wells for tears. It was an endless succession of girls all prettier than the last, all shoved in a competition pool with no winner.

I've never been them, not with *M's* on my tags. But that hardly matters anymore. My feet carry me father away from all of that with each stagnant step. I feel like a hamster on a wheel, running to nowhere.

Caged.

My eyes flit to the clock above me, telling me that 30 minutes has elapsed. I turn the treadmill off and slow my pace as it comes to a stop. My mom is just paranoid enough to bolt back to the room halfway through lunch, and I climb back up the several flights of stairs, ignoring the piercing fire in my quads.

I swipe the key through the door, but the light on the sensor flashes red. I try two more times before green pops up and stumble hurriedly into the room. When I see she isn't back yet, I collapse with relief on the bed. Sweat slides down my nose as I work my shoes free and tuck under the sheets. I wipe my face off on the covers a second before the door clicks and my mom walks into the room.

She sets her purse down on the desk and comes around to the side of the bed. "Willow?" I give my best impression of some sleep-drunk noise. "I'm back, and I brought you some food. How are you feeling?"

Of course she did. "I'm good. That nap was exactly what I needed. Not quite hungry yet."

"That's ok. I was looking just now and saw that there's a cute bookstore in town. Once you wake up a little, would you want to go there?" The fact that she's trying so hard sparks a new seed of guilt. My mom hates books, unless magazines count as literature. She's doing everything she can think of just to make me happy.

"Yea, that sounds fun. I could definitely use another book or two." Her face lights up and she claps her hand together. The seed grows into something with thorns and poisonous leaves.

In twenty minutes, we arrive in front of a used bookstore. I turn against the wind and hop quickly to the door. The inside is filled with golden light and the smell of inky pages unique to used bookstores. I trace spines of dusty volumes and glide between the stacks. The tingly feeling I get from being enveloped by thousands of stories pulses under my skin, like a humming of contentment. It works almost as well as exercising.

An hour passes as I collect words, cracking the spines of stiff novels and thumbing through well-read books. Sometimes I find notes written inside or letters written on the inside front cover. These books go in the keep pile, a small representation of how so many lives, so much humanness, exists in a single space, tucked carefully between stale pages.

My mom pays the cashier and a bell rings as we walk back into winter. Ghostly shadows slide across the ice as the sun dips behind the mountains. We grab some coffee, if only to keep our hands warm, and drive through the city streets. Porch lights flick on as dusk descends into the city. Buildings and trees are decorated in golden lights and wreaths of holly. Before long stars poke holes in the sky, illuminating the mountains' silhouette on the velvet tapestry.

We agree on dinner at a crowded Italian restaurant called Romano's Spaghetteria. My mom, predictably, orders the spaghetti, and I pick the house salad. Also predictable. We make small talk, chatting about Dante, our 13-year-old husky, then about Brian the Brainiac, my older brother. "He's doing great! Loves his classes, and his team is doing well. They don't play until spring, but he said they've been training daily." Brian the Brainiac is also Brian the Baseball player. Or Brian the Best. Or Brian the Stupidly-Perfect-Eldest-Child. I'm not picky.

"That's great. Good for him." Especially since he got in on a full ride, because Glenview isn't cheap. The dinner stretches over the better part of an hour. My mom eats almost all the spaghetti. I clear away a couple slices of cucumber and some lettuce to placate her worries.

With each passing minute I feel an invisible rope drag me back, pulling me out of this bubble and back to the hospital. She pays the bill and drives west, back through the mountains, past the river, up the dreadfully familiar driveway. I hug her goodbye at the front and walk back through the locked doors with Naomi, my freedom squashed between the industrial metallic bolts.

Everyone is in the common area watching some old movie I haven't seen, but I pass straight through after Naomi gives me the green light. I close my room door behind me and hit the floor, doing what I do best. The exercise lets the good day last a little bit longer. If I keep going, I can bridge the gap between now and leaving again tomorrow, pushing out the sucky reality for just a little longer.

There's a soft tap on the door, and it swings open. I'm caught, deer-in-headlights, completing a push up. I don't see how I can lie my way out of this. Pushing myself slowly off the ground, I come level with Emerson. He's standing in the doorway with a vacant expression, staring.

His eyes and cheeks droop like elastic that's been stretched too far. There's something behind his eyes that spikes my already elevated heart rate. Like a deadness. Thirty seconds of silence elapse with him standing in the frame, staring straight through me. "Em…" I walk slowly over to him, but he backs up and stumbles. It's then I notice he's wearing tennis shoes. We aren't allowed to wear them except to go to the gym, and I can't believe no one stopped him. "Em, please. Talk to me." What will happen if I can't reach him?

He pauses, dead center of the hallway, then turns on his heal and disappears. I race out of the room, but he's already gone. Is he going to tell someone? Rat me out? But the emptiness in his eyes, the tennis shoes, makes me think he's gone to a place no one can reach him. I remember the boy from my dreams, alone, desperate.

I lay on the thin sheets while my mind whirls. As my thoughts drift and my eyes begin to droop, fear isn't the only thing that follows me to sleep.

Chapter 12

"How high do you think it goes?"

"To the top. That sign back there called it 'summit road'." We wind up a steep, traversing pass. My mom grips the steering wheel with white knuckles and keeps her eyes glued firmly to the pavement. To the left, a boulder sticks out from the ground every few feet, and beyond that are hundreds of feet of air. The boulders aren't very confidence-inspiring in a match with a cliff. Still, up we climb.

We pass a blue minivan at a pullout, but other than that the road is empty. Trees stick out from the mountainside, clinging to the rock with shallow roots and tilting ominously down the slope. With each turn we ascend, more patches of snow cover the ground, though still polluted with grey soot. Finally, the ground levels, and the pavement gives way to dirt. The rental bounces across the ridge into a large pullout. The engine dies, and everything is *quiet*.

I step out of the car and walk to the edge. Mountain spines etch the horizon for miles, miles and miles, a river lazily carving out a valley between them. Clouds drips with gods' rays and a breeze ruffles my jacket. The only sound is the wind whistling though lone pines and my mom crunching the dirt to stand beside me. I can't hear any traffic, airplanes, lawn mowers, engines, music. Nothing.

The sunlight changes, bleeding through clouds in a symphony of colors. Spectacular pinks and reds swirl into vibrant oranges and periwinkle purple. Right now, right this moment, there's only this: the sky dripping color, millions of pine trees bowing in greeting, and my mom, breathing in every awe-inspiring moment. She drapes an arm across my shoulder as we stand and watch. Evening drapes over the mountains, shadowing each crevice of the valley, but the remnants of sunlight remain on our solitary peak.

The temperature drops, but we stay until Artemis makes landfall and clouds whisk over the inky sky. Together we walk silently back to the car, not wanting words to break the spell, but too frozen to stay any longer. The engine roars and heat trickles from the vents, as we begin our decent down the treacherous, unlit road.

When the ground finally flattens out both of us simultaneously relax. She laughs softly. "That was really beautiful, but let's not do that again."

I chuckle and say, "Yes. I completely agree. That was the

most terrifying drive ever, but hey, we're alive!" The laughter between us grows as we drive into the city.

"The man at the front desk told me about an ice sculpture exhibit that was supposed to open tonight. Do you want to go?"

"Sure!" Like those thousand-dollar ice-swans rich people get for their weddings? "Is it indoors?"

"It's all outside. They are supposed to be lit up too, for the holidays." Outside? Like in the fifteen-degree weather? Sounds *awesome*.

"Cool! Can't wait." The deeper we get into the city, the brighter it becomes. Ornamental lights decorate every bush and streetlamp, every stoop and tree branch. We pass the bookstore and parallel park a block from the ice show. I wrap my jacket tight around myself and curl my hands into the fleecy sleeves. We walk down the street and turn the corner. What we see is almost as amazing as the mountain sunset.

Towering sculptures of snow and ice are lit from within, illuminating them with green and blue glow. People pass between each one and snap pictures. I walk right up to a turret made of individual ice blocks. A blue light shines from inside, catching each block with dazzling radiance. It stands at least ten feet tall. My mom grabs my hand and steers me to the next, a five-foot tall lily with frosty petals. It's carved with incredible intricacy so that each petal is displayed in hyper-realistic relief.

My mom was right; this is awesome. "Good choice," I tell her. She smiles down at me with such warmth, I continue on to the next.

"Not too cold? We can grab some hot-chocolate if you want."

"Yeah, that sounds perfect." We meander for half an hour until my fingers turn to clubs and the tip of my nose feels frozen off. I step into a crowded café and inhale rich, nutty chocolate. The bell chimes as my mom shimmies into the store.

"Wow, look at that menu! Any idea what you want?" I shake my head. As we wait, my fingers begin to thaw, and I unzip my jacket. The menu is handwritten on a chalkboard and must hold fifteen different flavors of hot chocolate. There's hot chocolate with white chocolate, butterscotch, peppermint, caramel, hazelnut, and about a dozen others I've never conceptualized could go in hot chocolate.

"Can you get me a peppermint one? I can find us a seat."

"Sounds good to me." I leave my mom to weave through a host of crowded bodies, all migrating into this tiny café to escape the cold. There's a small two-seater by the window, and I push through the host of bodies to the table. I sink down into the chair and smile out the window. A giant ladybug sculpture is nearest us, glowing a deep scarlet. I can't believe I'm here. That this is happening. That I feel *happy*. For the first time in…weeks? Months? I cover my mouth to avoid grinning like an idiot at passing strangers, but the feeling stays.

My mom wades over and sets the drinks on the table. It strikes me that I'm not, like, momentarily happy. Like from excitement or from watching my favorite movie. The happiness flows from me, simply there, like it's doing to every other person in this shop. Right now, in this incredibly, mundane moment, I feel *normal*.

"What are you thinking about?"

"Nothing." I see her frown into her drink, just for a second. "I was thinking about how great this night is. Well, really the whole weekend. I'm so glad you came down! This has just been…really good. It's been amazing to see you."

She sniffs and stares at the window. "That's really sweet, baby. I've had a lot of fun with you too this weekend! It feels like it used to, doesn't it?" A tear rolls down her cheek, right here in the middle of this insanely packed café. I look away.

"Yeah. Yeah, it does."

She takes the lid off and blows away the steam. "It's getting late. Are you ready to head back?" *No.*

"Sure." We walk out into the bitter night, nearly slipping on a patch of black ice. The moment we get around the corner, both of us dive into the car. The air inside is just a few degrees warmer, but it only takes moments before streams of hot air hiss from the vents. I hold my fingers in front of them, soaking in the warmth. We pull out and meander back through the festive streets, savoring each minute.

"Wait. What is that? Is that—is it snowing?" White flakes swirl in the headlight beams and melt on the windshield. They gather in number and size, marble-like balls of white hitting the frozen pavement.

"I think you're right. It is! What a perfect way to end the night." I watch the frozen flakes pepper the asphalt, flitting around like white stars beneath a black sky. Despite the cold, a bubbling heat climbs up my neck. The pain reaches the base of my skull and explodes with fire. I press my face on the cold window, but the heat licks up to my ears.

It was snowing.

The memory is just there, at the base of my skull. My vision crowds with images of snow falling quietly on a dark night, the feeling of cold metal. It's *that* night. *The* night.

I realize that the black spot in my memory isn't black at all; it's white, white as snow. The heat trickles down my neck and disappears.

We pull into the entrance of Glenview, and the image dissolves. I turn to say goodbye, but Not-Jody opens the door.

"Sorry to cut it short, dear, but we need to get you inside. Mrs. Davidson, I am sincerely sorry."

I look back at my mom, stunned. Her eyes are wide with shock. I speak quickly as Not-Jody pulls me from the car. "Bye, thanks for everything. Have a safe fli—" Not-Jody shuts the door and ushers me inside. My mom waves after me, but it's cut off by the hefty door closing behind us.

"What's going on?"

She doesn't even look at me. Her face is straight, unreadable. "Nothing for you to worry about. Did you have a nice time with your mom?"

"Yeah it was—"

"Well, here we are." She unlocks the second set of doors and sweeps me inside. The common room is total chaos. Staff swarm around the room, and Hazel paces back and forth along the window-wall. All the other patients are in a tight knot by the TV. Zena walks over to me with tears streaming down her face. I search her face and find fear lined in every crevice.

"Zena, what's going on? Why is everyone panicking?"

"It's Em." Freezing dread fills my lungs, colder than the winter air. I move my eyes over the entire room but find no traces of him. Emerson. *What happened to Emerson?* "He ran."

Chapter 13

"What do you mean 'he ran'?"

Zena wipes her eyes. "He ran away. I don't know how, but he's gone, and they can't find him!" She pulls me in a very wet hug. "Willow, I'm so scared. He wasn't right; he hasn't been right." She pulls away and watches Hazel pace. "What if something happens to him?"

I follow her gaze to Hazel. *He ran. He ran. He ran.* My vision blurs, tears swelling in my eyes. How could he have left? But...I remember his shoes last night. The deadpan expression. This was planned. I look back at Zena, fresh tear tracks sliding down her face. The staff are all on high-alert, doing head counts every five minutes. Hazel is biting her nails, walking back and forth, back and freaking forth in some sort of manic frenzy. I *knew* something was wrong, but I did nothing.

Emerson has been right by my side since the moment I came here, and I left him to stew in his own malignant thoughts. Now he's gone, and *God,* I did nothing! He was struggling, and we let him. The boy from my dreams swims into my mind. I never even asked why he was here. I mean, it's common decency not to, but should I have, as a friend?

Because maybe then I would know what's going to happen. I would know if his first mission is to get high or get *really* high, like top of a bridge or building, high. Something is pulling at my feet, reeling me back to my room, begging for a release.

No. Not now. Please not now. I pull Zena over to a pair of beanbags and we sit, waiting, waiting, waiting. The room has lapsed into quiet, everyone afraid of the nasty, unspoken truth. How could we have not done anything more? I thought this place was locked down. I thought that's why Dr. Wilson and Dr. Patin and the entire host of annoying nurses were here: to spot something like that, to intervene. I thought that's what all of those shiny, framed, board-qualified certificates we for.

But…there's something else. I imagine myself, the weeks leading up to *that* night, the one I now know was filled with darkness and snow. It didn't matter what anyone else did or said: once my mind was made up, there was no backing out. It was going to happen regardless; it was just a matter of time.

"Alright everyone, it's time for bed," a nurse announces from the front. There's an immediate uproar of protesting.

"No way. We are staying here until we hear news of what's

really going on." Samson takes the lead. Everyone, minus Hazel, shouts in agreement. The nurse looks behind him for help, but no one is paying attention.

"Look, I know this is an anxious time for everyone, but nothing is going to change with you all out here or in your rooms."

Samson speaks up again. "That's bullshit and you know it."

The nurse drops his calm composure for one of clear agitation. "Alright, look. If everyone isn't in their rooms in the next sixty seconds, I'm taking away privileges." Is he related to Amanda somehow? Because this is patronizing at its finest. But, I must say, it works. Everyone, even Samson, stalks off angrily.

I pull Zena up and whisper out of the corner of my mouth. "Walkie-talkies." She sniffs and nods slightly, and we walk down the girls' hallway before parting ways.

Zena and I talk back and forth for several hours, unable to even think about sleep. "Heads up; checks." The static echoes, and I dive under the covers. There's the telltale click, then the door shuts again.

I click on the speaker. "Thanks. Are you sure he isn't

back yet? Maybe they brought him in and we didn't hear anything."

"My door is cracked. I would have heard something. Shit, Willow. It's 2:45. Why haven't they found him yet? What if—?"

"No. Let's not go there. He's fine. He's *fine*." I smooth my finger on the talk button in worry. She doesn't respond immediately, and the silence presses into my ears. I sigh into my pillow, willing him to be ok.

"You're right. He's fine. Are you tired at all?"

"No." Not until he's back. Not until he's ok.

"Me either. I really wanted to believe he was just pouting. I feel like such a *jerk*. He came to the gym yesterday. Did you know that? Em hates working out. I should have *realized*—"

"He made up his mind about it. We could have talked to him, but Emerson hasn't been the same for a while. Don't beat yourself up. We all missed it."

"Thanks, girl." The speaker dies, and I feign sleep. "Heads up; checks." Based on the nightstand clock, everyone is on fifteen minute checks, regardless of level status. The door swings open and shut.

"Thanks." Guilt presses the words from my mouth. "Hey, do you know why he's here? He doesn't talk about it in groups or anything." My voice is tight with fear, and I pray the speaker modulates it.

"Yeah. No. He was here a few days before me, but I never heard him talk about it. I mean, he's probably depressed, who isn't? But I don't know his history or anything." *Something* in his past clawed its way back. Why had I never asked? Maybe if we knew, we could have done something, said something. He wouldn't have been so alone.

"Same. I wonder—"

"What? What is it?" I put my hand over the speaker and listen. It's muffled, but I can make out banging sounds. Voices.

"Did you hear that?"

"Hear wha—?" Her voice is cut off by yelling. I tear off the sheets and sprint out of the room, knocking into someone in the hallway. "Ow, Willow that was my foot."

"Sorry, it's dark out here." Other faces pop out from the doors as Zena and I creep down the hallway. The banging sounds get louder as we edge closer.

"Stop!" The sounds of heavy panting. "Get off me!" Zena turns to me and mouths 'Em!'. We walk into the edge of the common room, and a mixture of horror and relief floods through me.

Emerson is struggling with four nurses. He gets to his feet and lunges forward, but they just pull him back. Terror ripples through every syllable, every pained expression. "No! Please, *please!*" They wrestle him down the hallway, but his voice carries into the common area. "Stop! Let—me—*go!*" His legs are kicking out, wild. Desperate. Two nurses grab his feet and carry him into a room. He's pleading, frantic, begging them to let him go. To let him freaking go. They don't close the door, but his screams die. Everything is quiet. Still. No one moves.

I now notice everyone is out of their rooms, standing somberly. Because what are you supposed to say when you just watched your friend get dragged into a room and sedated? How is that fair? The fact looms over us like a threat, smothering us with panic. Zena's face is wet with fresh tears. Piper has her hand over her mouth. Across the hallway, I can see Jeremy, standing frozen in shock. And somewhere in the depths of that awful room is Emerson, limp and drooling.

Alone. Again.

Three nurses, straightening their scrubs, walk out from the room. When they look up and see us, I expect more shouting. Instead, the same nurse who told us off earlier just sighs. "I'm sorry you all had to see that. But it's late, and the best thing for everyone right now is to try and get some sleep. You'll have time to process everything tomorrow." He walks over to the nurse's station and collapses into a seat, not even waiting to watch us march back. But we do, not because anyone's going to sleep, but because if we remove ourselves from the scene of the crime, maybe it didn't happen.

I get back to my room and close the door. The walkie-talkie is on my nightstand, but it stays silent. Staring at the ceiling, I lay back into the bed, resting my hands on my stomach. Again and again I watch Emerson, with sickening clarity, claw his way past the nurses. I can see his arms stretch for the door, his torso lifted off the ground. He had dirt smudged on his nose, but other than that there was nothing to give evidence of where he'd been.

I think he only had a week or two left at Glenview. What was so bad that he couldn't wait? What demons drove him from here with that much urgency? Who knows how much longer they'll keep him here now. As the hours yawn past and sunlight peeks through my window, I think that Emerson might be the only person in this entire building who actually slept.

Chapter 14

When Dr. Patin breezes into group, she doesn't smile. No greeting. She sits in her usual chair at the front and crosses her ankles. I watch her pick an invisible piece of lint from her skirt, but my eyes revolve to the black, cracked leather chair across the circle. Emerson's chair.

"Good morning, everyone. I know having this group at the normal time seems cruel, especially as it's clear none of you slept, but we have to remember how important it is to discuss how we are feeling. To be open with one another." She clasps her hands around her knee and observes us. No one moves. No one even displays the usual anxious fluttering. Dr. Patin allows the silence to build, allows our feeling to slowly churn. Up our throats. Out of our mouths. Staining the already marked floor.

"If no one would like to volunteer to go first, then we can go in a circle. Zena, why don't you lead us off?" Zena doesn't stir or make any sign that she'd been spoken to. Her eyes burn holes in the carpet. She wraps her arms around herself, trying to shield away that nasty truth.

"I wish he would have said something. I wish *I* would have said something to him." She lifts her gaze and meets each of our eyes. "We are a community. We are supposed to support one another, since all of us are going through the same shitty thing." Her eyes land on Emerson's chair. "But we didn't. We failed Emerson." Everyone shifts as the truth slithers over them. Wrapping around their throats.

"Feeling comfortable with one another and maintaining a strong sense of community are of extreme importance. I also want to stress that while healthy friendships are encouraged, no one here is responsible for Emerson's actions." Hot, white anger boils under my skin, and a tongue of fire lashes out like a surge of energy.

"Then who is responsible exactly?" I spew the words out. "How is guilt not deserved when I saw someone suffering, and did nothing? There is no excuse for that."

Dr. Patin leans forward and tilts her head, making her bun sway a little. "Everyone here is capable of making mistakes, by default of being human. There will always be opportunities to help and support others who need it, and we are responsible for acting or not acting on those opportunities. There is no fault on any of you, however, for the choices Emerson made. Those belong to Emerson, and Emerson alone." She uncrosses her legs and examines everyone. "While you all are here, and in the time following your stay, I want to point out that before you can take care of others, you must first take care of yourself. It is essential everyone here knows that."

Dr. Patin surveys each of us, waiting for signs of confirmation. Only Zena doesn't nod.

"That's a nice thought, but if we got to him, if I just *talked* to him, he might not have left." Something like courage rises from some deep, deep ravine. *Why* it has to be courage and not fear or the desire to stay quiet, I don't know. I take a deep breath, and speak candidly.

"That's not always true." My palms start to sweat as every head snaps in my direction. Is your heart supposed to beat that fast? *Tell me* there's an antidote to courage? "Sometimes, when a person gets to that place, a place where they are so far gone, no one can pull them back. Not any amount of support or encouragement. It's…it's like a virus that has to run its course. We could have, and should have done more for Emerson, but I don't think it would have changed the outcome. All we can do now is do what we should have: be there. Don't let him feel alone."

I look to Zena. She's wearing a small smile, but behind her eyes is something certain, firm. Like resolve. It's a look so specific that her face shouldn't fit exactly with the lines and grooves set there. But it does, and I know that whatever is in Zena's history is something of horrible trauma. That resilience in her eyes is well worn.

"Sometimes our emotions carry us to a place so dim, it can feel impossible to even imagine light." Dr. Patin moves her eyes to me, and I nod. "In those times, love and friendship can act as guides to help lead that person from the darkness. Support and kindness are thoughtful ideas to help Emerson, and we have to keep in mind his perspective. Emerson is likely to be overwhelmed right now, so large amounts of up-front encouragement, while full of good intentions, might not be received as such. I promise to let him know how much all of you care about him and are rooting for his recovery. I'm also available after group, if anyone would like to talk. Thank you for being open and honest with me, and yourselves. I think we can end group a little early today, if no one has any objections?" The silence is the sweetest music, and everyone piles out with lowered heads, congregating in the common area to rest our usual post-group emotion hangovers.

I sit down in the moldy couch next to Zena. Her blond hair is tied back in a messy bun, and lose strands fall on her face. For Zena, this is a glaring sign of distress. "Hey, how are you holding up?"

She shrugs. "I'm fine. But I swear to God, Willow, I'm going to get Em back on track even if I have to stay here for a year." Her eyes follow Dr. Patin walking to the nurse's station.

"I know. And I'll be right there with you."

She cracks a smile and rolls her eyes. "Well, yeah! You better, because if you go and pull an Em, I'll kill ya." Zena aims a finger pistol at me, and I laugh, tossing a grimy pillow over her head. "Girl, you've got to work on that aim. You're worse than Jeremy."

And as easily as breathing, we fall back into our usual banter, showing off Amanda impressions (as she scolds Samson for looking glum) and brainstorming increasingly large small acts of rebellion. Even in the middle of every messed up part of this screwed up week, this dose or normalcy keeps it all doable. Survivable. If it only wasn't a Monday, and sixty torturous minutes weren't waiting for me in one horribly comfortable chair. I enjoy the extra time with Zena and the others without so much of a thought about exercising. My eyes, however, stay glued to the boys' hallway, waiting for the smallest flash of red.

Webber is a few minutes late today, which I hope means this weekly torture will be a few minutes shorter. He swivels in the leatherback chair, rolling the pen. The gesture sends red flags popping up behind my eyes.

"Good afternoon, Willow."

"'Afternoon." I brace for an Emerson interrogation. My spine is so stiff that it doesn't even touch the seat, and I sit on my hands to avoid fidgeting.

"What would you like to talk about today?"

"I don't know." My back starts to ache.

He sets the pen down to properly scrutinize me. "Did you do the homework from last week?" With a jolt of shame, I realize I did do it. Not that the answer is shrink-approved.

"Nope." Webber, who can spot a lie before it reaches my mouth, leans forward on his legs and sighs.

"Why do you think you are here?" No, let's not do this. Let's *please* not do this. I thought we had reached an understanding with this topic. He doesn't ask, and I don't lie.

"What do you mean?"

His eyes bore into mine, but his posture doesn't change. "You know what I mean. Why are you here?"

"Because I don't have a choice." My breathing thins out

into something shallow and insubstantial, opposing the rapidly beating rhythm of my heart.

Webber doesn't seem mad, but the tone of his voice is firm. "Try again."

"Well, it's true. I wouldn't be here if it was up to me." I don't say what I really mean, but a wrinkle grows between his eyes. My subtext is clear.

"Willow," he presses, "why are you here?" I move my eyes to the window, memorize the brown shrubbery and dead leaves. I count the cars in the parking lots, watch sparrows hop from tree branch to tree branch. The image begins to swim, darken. As if my eyes pull in the outside, Webber's office drops ten degrees. "Remember, you are safe here."

Small white cannonballs explode against concrete.

Webber grabs his pen.

There's metal under my fingers, bitterly cold. They start to sting.

My shirt touches the seat-back.

"I think there's a problem with your record keeping if you don't already have an answer to that question." My nose pricks with cold. A snowflake falls between my eyes. The image starts to surface, but something isn't right. It's like a smudge of dirt on a photograph. The memory is there, in sharp focus, but

I can't see what's under the dirt. *What am I not remembering?*

"I want to hear it from you." He rolls the pen back and forth. There are callouses on his fingers.

I shrug. "I have depression. Like half of America. It's a super common, super mundane thing." My hands slide out and pick at my legs, digging into the copious fat, and the image begins to melt away.

"Depression is the most common mental illness, that is true. But half of America isn't hospitalized for it." His eyes follow the path of my fingers, and he frowns.

"Well, they probably don't have overly-concerned parents, either. Lucky me." I bring my eyes back to his, which are searching my face, giving the impression he knows more under the BS than I would like. Under my sleeves, I feel goosebumps pop up, from cold or fear I can't tell.

"Why do you think your parents were so concerned?" He is *relentless*. My stomach rumbles, and my hands start to shake. I let the hypoglycemia charge through me like courage and spin some of the finest BS.

"They're parents. It's their job to be paranoid and worried. One time I came home from school five minutes later than normal, and my mom was already calling me, convinced I'd been in an accident or kidnapped.

"You don't think cutting or burning are things to be concerned about?" I glare at him, forcing as much heat into that stare as I can muster. My eyes are slits of pure loathing. Unfortunately, Webber doesn't so much as flinch. "What about suicide?"

I read a quote once, on some depressed, emo website that said it better than any way I thought of: "If you knew what went on in my head, the cuts would be nothing." Webber wants me to talk about the behaviors, not what fueled them. Self-harm is only a manifestation of getting rid of the suckiness inside. The means to an end.

This freaking place. Now I sound like the shrink. "They didn't know about that stuff until later. Until recently." If this is psychological chess, I'm not so much losing as completely trapped. The look on Webber's face doesn't argue the contrary. What is the problem with a secret or two? Can't I keep some part of my innermost garbage in the dark?

"Until when?" Don't do this, Webber. Don't even think about it.

"You know perfectly well when. If you're waiting for me to tell you, it's not going to happen, because I don't care for redundancy." He brings his hands together and, I kid you not, actually twiddles his thumbs. In his eyes is the slightest spark of amusement, like I know I just lost the game but sent the chess pieces flying.

"Well, I'm curious. Why did it take them so long to find out? Suicide attempts and self-harm come from months or years of struggling."

My eyes trace down the gilded lettering of his books. "I didn't want them finding out, clearly. It helped that they ignored whatever bits they caught on to." My fingers shake as they press in further, and I unwind into the pain.

"So you carried all of this alone. No one knew what you were doing or how you were feeling? That must have been exhausting." He squints at my hands, scratching fervently, and pulls his eyebrows together.

I shrug. "Not really."

Webber sighs and leans back in the chair. The pen rests on his notepad beneath half a page of comments, and he massages the pinched skin on his fingers. "There's a quote, by one of my favorite poets. It says, 'There is no greater feeling for the human spirit than to have survived. And there is no greater defeat to the human spirit than to be surviving'. What do you think about that?"

I think whoever came up with it should be chucked in a psych ward. "Well, I don't know. I'm not *surviving* anything."

Because I'm not planning on leaving this place alive. No amount of sessions with Webber is going to cure me and all my insanity.

"I would like you to give it some more thought between now and next Monday. We're out of time for today, but Thursday is family therapy with your dad. Think about what you might want to discuss." I give him a tight-lipped smile and nod. "Also, the staff have been impressed by the hard work and progress you've made, so you are officially on level two."

Excitement leaps in my chest, but I manage to keep a straight face. "Ok, thanks." Webber can't know how much this makes me happy, because I resent everything about this place, Webber included. My feet carry me out of the office and down to the common room where Amanda and a round of orthostatic vitals are waiting to puncture my joy with one tight squeeze.

Chapter 15

Emerson stays holed up in his room with an hourly rotation of staff for company. His absence leaves a space, this depthless pit sucking me down into it. I fill it up with anything and everything to avoid falling down into that shared blackness. I stuff it with the calories I hide from nurses, the number of hours I exercise, the hypoglycemia and sweating and weakness that chase me from bed in the morning. I pile it so full of the gallons of water washing through my organs that it can't possibly have room to eat me too.

Tuesday has all of us killing time in the common area, waiting to get stripped bare in shame group. My legs shake under my weight, but I refuse to sit. I keep moving, standing, walking, finding excuses not to stay still. The depression isn't gone so much as diluted. On a brief hiatus. But something keeps me coming back to the floor in my room. To tossing the replacement shakes.

All I can think about is the way I feel, right now. Hollow. Tired. Light. Not so much happiness but direction runs through my veins into every muscle fiber, fulfilling purpose once robbed by depression. My brain is racked with an endless secession of numbers: my vitals, the back of nutritional labels, calories in, calories out, how much I worked out. The tangibility is delicious.

"Group time, everyone!" We amble into the familiar chairs like trained dogs. Megan and Tyler, a couple of local grad students, lead Tuesday shame groups each week as part of a practicum requirement. Megan is at least 5'9", and has her brown hair down and wavy. Tyler wears a pink button-down shirt and a pair of jeans. He tucks his hands in his pockets and smiles at us casually, like we're all just pals hanging out between class.

"Good afternoon everyone! How are all of you on this *fine* Tuesday?" Tyler doesn't wait for a response, knowing it's only futile, and launches forward. "For today, I need everyone to make sure you have a hard surface to write on. If you need to grab books from your rooms, go right ahead." There's murmuring of dissent, and a few people shuffle out of their seats. There's an old desk that backs up to my chair, so I watch Megan pass out pieces paper to everyone. She hands one to me with what looks like the outline of a gingerbread man.

Megan puts a bucket of markers in the middle of our oval, all looking like they spent an eternity in a kindergarten classroom. Jeremy and Piper slide back into the room, and Tyler beams at their reentry. "Excellent, excellent. Today we're going to get a little crafty. I would like you guys, and gals, for the next fifteen minutes, to write down any shame thoughts and beliefs you have about yourself in and around the figure on your sheets. The markers are here in the middle, take as many as you need."

Predictably, everyone scrambles toward the single container. Hazel and I remain until everyone settles back down to grab ours. I roll a red marker between my fingers in mockery of Webber and swivel around in my chair. The desk has ridges and grooves in it, so the marker bumps over the paper sloppily. I look at my little gingerbread man, but don't write anything besides my name. Glancing over my shoulder, I watch everyone consumed in marring their paper with libel.

My gingerbread man stays wordless except for my name. I uncap the marker and start coloring in the arms and down each leg. The color bleeds out past the lines. The marker ticks fresh wounds across the poor man's face, into his chest and belly until the whole thing is red. All the words stay unwritten. Burden. Selfish. Broken. Worthless. Failure. The words circle faster and faster like a cyclone, spinning around my gravity. New words break through into the familiar mantra: stupid, fat, ugly, lazy, pain. They get swirled into the ferocious winds and bullet-like rain, shredding my skin until I'm just like the gingerbread man; red and bleeding.

Tyler's voice cuts through the howling winds. "Alright, time's up! Now, before we share, I want you to turn over your paper and pass it to the person on your right." He waits as our private, most secret beliefs are handed over and continues. "For the remaining time, I want you to write what you think and believe of the person who just handed you their paper. Take your time, and be thoughtful."

Because my luck sucks, or the universe is giving me the middle finger, Piper is on my right and snatches the paper greedily. I watch her for a moment, making sure she doesn't flip it over, and start writing on Samson's.

Words like "hope" and "passion" and "leader" flow easily onto the paper. I fill up the space with promises of talent and a fiery, inner strength. One of his shame-beliefs bleeds through the paper, and even backward, the words are clear. *Never enough*. This amazing guy, so full of life and energy and determination and *Samson* can't see himself besides disappointment and athletic failures. I trace the marker over the words so many times that *Enough* boldly bleeds back through the paper, probably obscuring the other words of hate.

"Well done, everyone. That's all the time we have for now, but hang on to your papers! We'll go over them next week." Tyler's enthusiasm couldn't be more juxtapose to the purpose of *shame* group. I hand the paper back to Samson and accept mine from Piper, who I think actually looks smug. The red marker smacks its companions in the box, and I crumple the paper on my way out. "I want everyone to have an excellent week! Stay grand, my friends."

I file out into the common area, but a mane of red hair comes pelting at me. "Willow!" Emerson pulls me into a crushing hug. I tuck my head into his shoulder and squeeze back.

"Boundaries! Both of you!" Amanda's voice carries through the room, but Emerson hangs on a minute more before pulling away. His face is pink with embarrassment.

"Can—can I talk to you?" I channel my inner Zena and punch him in the arm.

"Yes, of *course!* Can you…?" I motion my head to the nurses' station, but he shakes his head.

"Line of sight. At least I'm not on one-to-one anymore. I will never again take bathroom privacy for granted." He smiles that amazing, goofy smile, and I lead him to a pair of beanbags in the back. Amanda glances in our direction, but doesn't say anything.

"Talk to me. How are you?" *What happened?* His face blushes to a red that clashes magnificently with his hair.

"Look, I'm really sorry. It's…I haven't been…" The sentence hangs as he struggles to find the right words.

"You can tell me anything. I promise, no judgement."

He looks out the window. We do a lot of window staring in this place. "I haven't been open with you about my past." I don't say anything, let him compose his thoughts. "I tell people I have depression, which is technically true, but it isn't the entire truth. It's so stupid, pathetic, really…" Emerson lets out a heavy sigh, and brings his eyes to mine. "I have bulimia. Or had. I'm in recovery, I guess. I don't go to the gym because I'm not supposed to exercise. I know what you're thinking; it's a *girl* illness. What guy gets an eating disorder?"

I shake my head. "Emerson, I wasn't thinking that at all. I'm so sorry. I've been such an awful friend. You've clearly been dealing with a lot, and completely on your own. Is that what you've been struggling with lately? Has it been…worse?"

He wrings out his hands, tapping his foot anxiously on the carpet. "Yes. No. It's just, when I saw you, it made me remember, and I can't—I can't…" Emerson jumps up and walks around the beanbag. He brings his hands behind his head and stares at the floor. Fear reflects off his wide eyes. "I can't go back there. You don't know…you don't understand what it was like."

"Go back where?" I want to hug him, or tell him not to think about it, but I can see he needs to get the words out. He has to.

"I can't go back. Not there. Please." Emerson closes his eyes and tips his head to the ceiling, chanting, "please, please, please" under his breath. I have no idea who he's talking to, because it definitely isn't me, but whoever it is terrifies him deeply. He wraps his arms around himself and starts walking in frantic circles, trying to outstrip this invisible tormentor. I have never seen anything so sad.

"Emerson, it's ok. I'm right here." He takes a deep breath and walks slowly back to the beanbag.

"I'm sorry. I know I'm being crazy right now. But it's *him* I can't go back to. Ed. He started coming back when I saw you. You know about Ed."

I shake my head. "No, I don't. Who is Ed?"

"Geez, Willow. What are you doing here? *Ed.* E.D." When I don't recognize the name, he says incredulously, "Eating Disorder. Ed is short for Eating Disorder."

My tone comes out colder than I intended. "Why would I have known that? And what do you mean it got worse when you 'saw me'?"

"That's why you're here, isn't it? I've seen you restricting, body checking. It, I guess *triggered* me, for lack of a better word. Brought back some old habits. But how long have you secretly been working out? Do you know how dangerous that is?"

Frustration works heat from my muscles. "Dangerous? Are jumping jacks *dangerous*? And no, I'm here for depression. And I guess self-harm. Emerson, I really wasn't trying to make you uncomfortable; I didn't know." I press my fingers between my eyes and take a breath. "Look, I'm sorry. I don't want to argue. I've really missed you. So has Zena, though she's too proud to admit it. Can we just…I don't know…push a reset button or something?"

Emerson looks like he has more to say but just nods. "Yeah. That sounds good. Where is Zena, by the way?"

"Family therapy." He cringes, and I laugh. Smiles creep up both of our faces.

"That's unfortunate."

"Very."

He collapses back in the beanbag. "Ugh, I have mine

tomorrow. My mom is going to *murder* me." He smiles wider, masking the dread beneath.

"Just your mom?"

"Yeah." He wrinkles his nose. "Dad isn't really in the picture."

"I'm sorry. I didn't know." I shift to see him better.

"Don't be. I'm not. Anyway, you up for a game of Frosty?" I nod, and he grabs a deck from the arts table.

We play through dinner, which he harps on me for missing, and on into the evening. Zena joins in, then Samson and Jeremy. By the end of the night, the five of us, plus Anthony, are gathered in a circle, slapping down cards and raucous with laughter. That is one of the stereotypes they got right; card games are an Olympic sport in psychiatric hospitals. I guess it isn't *always* terrible here.

I call it a night around 10:00 and headed back to my room. The cool sheets feel silky against my flushed skin, and I curl beneath them. My hands work of their own accord, pinching the copious skin on my stomach, then my arms. I fall asleep thinking *too much, I'm too much.*

Chapter 16

"Time to get up, Willow. You have family therapy in fifteen minutes." I crack open an eye and spot Anthony leaning against the door frame.

"Don't remind me. Can't it be Friday? We can just skip it…"

He starts laughing and concedes, "You can if you want, but Zena's been threatening to come in here with a bucket of water if you don't get up soon." Anthony shoves off the frame and disappears back into the hall. He shouts, loud enough for me to hear, "She's all yours, Zena. Go crazy."

Zena's shrill tones jar me from the last webs of sleep. "As a crazy person, I take offense to that!" Her feet thump down the hallway, closer and closer. "Get up, girl! You missed breakfast again, and Amanda is *not* happy."

"You realize that's just more incentive to stay in bed, right?"

She sits on the foot of my bed and teases, "You know, I think I *will* get a bucket of water."

I chuckle and swing my legs over the side of the bed, massaging out some fabulous psych hospital bedhead. "Good luck finding one. Probably considered a 'drowning hazard'."

"Very funny, Little Miss Sunshine. Come on." She pulls me up, and we wade back to the common room. "You know, Em told me yesterday. Why he's here."

"Yeah, he told me when you had therapy. I had no idea."

"Same! I'm just glad he opened up about it. He talked a bit about you too."

My eyebrows shoot up. "Oh? What did he say?" Zena rolls her eyes, a very practiced expression.

"He*llo*? He is worried! Girl, maybe you do need that beauty rest." She spots Amanda storming over and dive-bombs a couch. "Good luck!" Amanda shoots me a stern look and lightly grabs my elbow.

"Let's get your vitals. And where were you during breakfast this morning?" Where was I? Like they don't keep the exact GPS coordinates of all of us. I follow her over and hold out my arm.

"Um, sleeping? Breakfast is way too early." She makes a "humph" sound and scribbles down my blood pressure.

"And if I get you a shake, will you drink it? I see here that you've been refusing them daily. You know the more you do that, the longer you'll be here." Alright, if the fact that it's still morning or that I have family therapy isn't enough, Amanda's hovering seals the deal. Today the asylum gods are *not* pleased.

"I'm not hungry in the morning. Half the people here sleep through breakfast, but none of them are given replacement shakes."

She sets down the clipboard and stands over me with her arms crossed. Uh-oh. "Your vitals today are the same as when you nearly *fainted*. This isn't something to mess around with, Willow. I better see you eat a full lunch, or else we're going to need to talk."

I raise my eyebrows at her and give a sickly sweet smile. "Got it. Am I good to go here? Don't want to be late for therapy."

She nods and sets my chart on the desk. I watch Amanda stalk over in Emerson's direction with an ominously looking Styrofoam cup. I throw him a sympathetic smile, but he buries himself further into the sofa. If it can sense Amanda, my stomach grumbles, betraying the hunger writhing inside.

But this physical pain, the hunger gnawing at my stomach, is at least something I can influence. It's the only liberty I have left here. Not my own emotions, not when I get to wake up or how much time I get to myself. I know that regardless of the threats, lunch just isn't going to happen, not with *smaller, smaller, smaller* chanting in my head.

My feet carry me down Webber's hallway, feeling heavier with each step. His door is ajar; I knock on the frame. "Come on in." He's jotting a last minute note with that infamous pen, and doesn't look up immediately. Webber wears a blue polo shirt and black slacks, fancy shoes and a tie to match. He must have dressed for treatment team meetings. "Good afternoon," he says. "How are you?"

I sit rigidly in the too-comfortable chair and mutter, "Fine." The dial tone echoes in the small office, and we wait. One ring. Two. *Please don't pick up. Please don't pick up.*

"Hello? Is this Dr. Webber?"

"Yes, hello, David. I have Willow with me for today's session." There's a brief pause in the line.

"Oh, yes! Hello, Willow! How have you been?" *How have I been?* I'm trapped in a crazy house and haven't felt fresh air for almost a week. Does anyone actually respond with "good"?

"I'm good. And you?"

"Oh, I'm very well! Business is excellent; I got a new client this past Monday. Very exciting stuff. Of course, the vacation was just wonderful! Park City got two feet of snow while we were out there." A sucking sensation begins somewhere in my chest, like someone pulled the drain on a bathtub. Cold water clings to my skin.

"That sounds great. When was your vacation?" He happily fills in the details, oblivious to the coldness, settling into me with intimate familiarity.

"We left about a week ago. Came back early yesterday for your therapy session today. I was sorry to leave; the skiing was just terrific!" Shame blooms in my empty stomach, unfurling into the copious space. He was here, in Utah. Half an hour away. I guess skiing is more of a vacation than visiting his suicidal daughter in the hospital. Feeling the love, Dad. Truly.

"Well, I'm very sorry to cut your trip short. It sounds like you were having a really good time."

"Yes, we were. Well, such is life. I couldn't miss such an important family obligation." Of course not. How else could he lay the guilt on me? Webber's pen is flying across the page, ink smudging his wrist. He senses the lull of chatter and looks up, his brows furrowed almost to his nose. Webber, per usual, makes a roadmap of my facial expression and body language, scanning for signs of distress. But that ship has sailed, leaving blankness and apathy in its wake.

"David, how would you describe your relationship with Willow?" The speaker stays silent for almost a full twenty seconds. My eyes trace the familiar spines of books.

"I would say we have a good relationship. There isn't anything in particular I see as problematic."

Webber rubs the pen-worn spots on his fingers. "I see. Could you point out one positive and one negative about your relationship with Willow?" The line goes silent again, like he's actually thinking in that emotionless, robotic brain.

"Well, we have a very easy relationship. Some conflict, but not much more than average parent and teen, I expect. A negative? I don't see Willow apply herself very much. She's so full of talent, she could do anything! But she prefers her time spent neglecting her homework or sleeping."

Somewhere in the apathy, white hot anger breaks through, rising with words and tumult. "Dad, he asked for a negative on our relationship, not a flaw about my character. And in case you weren't aware, those things are symptoms of *depression*. You know, the thing you chucked me in here for?" My breathing is coming out shallow and fast, fueled by adrenaline.

It doesn't go unnoticed. "Willow, what are you feeling right now?"

"Nothing." Webber gives me a sarcastic look that says,

really? "If our relationship doesn't have problems, it's because we don't have a relationship to begin with. He seems perfectly fine with that, and so am I." This knocks a good thirty seconds of silence into the room. A *long* thirty seconds. I look down at my feet, smooth my palms over my washboard thighs.

"What is going through your head right now, David?"

"Well, I'm just so sorry Willow feels that way. I happen to think we have a very strong relationship. I have no idea where that thinking came from." More shame. More guilt. Classic Dad manipulation; make me and my accusations seem crazy, while elevating himself. Surprisingly, I think Webber sees through it. At least, that's what I'm assuming that page of notes indicates.

"You're right. What was I even thinking?" My tone is saturated with angry sarcasm, and I glare at the dead shrubs outside. "We have such a stellar relationship you would rather fly all the way out here and go skiing than visit. How stupid of me not to see that you did this because we are *close*." I'm waiting for Webber to intervene, moderate or tell me to *take deep breaths*, but he doesn't. He stays tight lipped, looking between me and the phone, apparently feeling like this needs to happen.

My father's voice comes through the speaker with a sternness that could rival Amanda. "Willow, you are confused about what happened. I have a very demanding job, and thought I deserved a short vacation. The number of hours I work every day are the ones that can afford your treatment, that will get you a car and pay for college. I thought you, of all people, would be more grateful." Of course. I haven't expressed enough gratitude for what he calls *love*.

This is the problem with his problem; it's subtle. He's not yelling at me or calling me names. At his house, I could greet him in the morning, and without another word, he would tell me how he slept, or didn't. The dreams he had. What he planned to have for breakfast. How I was lazy for waking up so late, regardless of the time. All without even the reciprocal *good morning*.

It's a kind of living that chipped at my existence. The longer I stayed there, the longer I felt myself blend into the wall paper. I started to wonder that if I ran into someone, would they even feel it? If I spoke, would anyone hear me? It was a kind of living that didn't make me feel like I didn't matter, it made me wonder if I *ever* mattered. Oh, boy, did depression love that.

"Willow?" Webber's voice is gentle. Worried.

"I don't have anything to say. He got all the finer points." Blood starts whooshing in my ears, silencing the rest of the conversation. I can see Webber look at me a couple times, waiting to contribute something, but I don't say anything. I'm staring out the window at the same dead bushes, waiting for depression to wrap its arms around me.

But it doesn't.

Not so much as a flicker of sadness. A burning desire chases away the shame in my stomach. It's heat with direction, and I follow it. The path meanders through a wasteland of *empty*, promising that with every calorie I deny, the feeling will grow. I imagine myself in my room, drained by the physical exhaustion of exercising, and an excited shiver runs through me. Like there's something else, living just beneath my skin. The meaning is clear: with it, I'm safe. I'm invulnerable to depression. Just the *thought* brings goosebumps to my skin.

Webber ends the phone call and turns to me, waiting. But this liquid purpose gives me confidence I can outlast the silence. His stare burns into my face, but after a minute I still haven't spoken. "Willow, what are you thinking? You've been quite for a while now." My eyes flit to the analog clock above the door.

A smile creeps up my face. "I'm hungry. I'm thinking

about lunch, which is in five minutes." This has the opposite effect of assuaging his worry, but I don't care. I'm *light*, above all of this. He says something, but it soars over my head and out the door. I follow it, walking into the common area where everyone, except Emerson, are gathered for lunch. The feeling flits and crawls under my skin like there's something just beneath the dermis waiting to escape.

I think I know how to let it.

The cafeteria smells like refried beans and too many different foods. I select a tall glass of water and a banana and slide into a chair between Zena and, against my better judgement, Amanda. Amanda takes one look at my lunch and shakes her head. "I don't think so. Come on, let's get you an actual meal."

I have enough anxiety in this stupid place without the unwanted maternal smothering. Zena loads a spoonful of chili but makes no notice of the rising tension. "This is fine. I'm not that hungry right now."

"Hu-uh. If you don't come with me to get more food, then I'm going to pick it all out for you." She stands up and heads toward the pile of trays.

"Here's the thing. I'm not hungry, and seeing more food in

front of me isn't going to give me a sudden burst of appetite. You can get more food, but I'm not going to eat it, as I'm *not hungry*." I can sense a few other people watching me, and my face burns. Why does this have to be such a big deal? I don't *want* this. How am I supposed to eat anyway with everyone staring? If only I could take the banana back to my room…but Amanda would see, and I doubt that would go over well.

"Willow," Amanda leans in and says quietly, "we are going to have to talk about this after lunch."

"There's nothing to talk about." A sly voice whispers in my other ear: *stay empty*. With Amanda hovering and half the cafeteria staring, the little appetite I have vanishes. And, you know what? It feels *good*. So, *so* good. The empty high makes me feel like I'm filled with helium, that I can ascend above whatever reprimand is waiting. And even though I have friends here, for the first time since I arrived,

I don't feel alone.

Or depressed.

I'm not thinking about *that* night.

Or family therapy.

I feel giddy. Electric. I'm so high above everything, so *light*, that all of these anxieties look like nothing more than insignificant specks. The helium fills every available space and crevice, squeezing into every hollow I've created, until I'm afloat with nothingness.

Before, to feel the beautiful burn in my legs, I'd have to do endless lunges and burpees. Now they cry out just from walking, tiring completely on the journey back to the common area. *Good. Now you can't be caught exercising.*

Thankfully, after lunch Amanda gets swept away by Piper with some complaint, and I have a few minutes of freedom. I spend them walking around the common area. I have too much energy to sit. My focus slides and shifts away like running drops of water, so I can't concentrate on anything.

All I see is the floor and the falling snow outside and the numbers spinning around and around. The numbers crawl and divide and tuck into every fissure of my brain like a colony of ants. Calories in, calories out, the number I'm not allowed to see on the scale, checking and rechecking the same calculations because that thing inside demands that everything is *perfect*. Flawless.

Black spots replace snowflakes, and a wave of dizziness sends me leaning into the windows. I can feel something within me, just above my stomach, just below my lungs, purr with satisfaction. *This is good. This means you're doing it right.*

And as if every wasted calorie is a stroke of luck, I never

do get that confrontation with Amanda. Emerson doesn't nag at me, and looks to be enjoying himself. No one misses me at evening check-in.

I'm untouchable.

When I get back to my room, I spot a Jolly Rancher on my bed. A blue one. It has to be from Emerson. I don't know how or why, but I know it's from him. A single piece of candy, sitting innocently in the middle of my bed. I toss it on my desk and thump down into the covers.

At first, I don't understand the purpose of it. I've seen him plenty of times; he could have just handed it to me. And it would have been much easier than slipping down the girls' hallway and back out without raising suspicion.

But the longer it sits on my desk, the more I imagine what it would taste like. Hard against my teeth, blue-raspberry lavishly coating my mouth. My palms start to sweat when I imagine the sugar dissolving into my bloodstream. My hands vibrate each time I think about twisting off the wrapper, tossing it in my mouth.

And I know this is exactly what Emerson was trying to accomplish. Damn if I don't stare at that piece of candy all night.

Chapter 17

I want to say that my clothes feel looser, or that my ribcage expands like a skeletal frame, but I'm more or less the same. Still wishing my brother's medium hoodie fit like a large. Still feeling the sleeves of my shirts tighten around my skin. My cheekbones aren't hollow in some sort of sick glamour, or my eyes sunken and gaunt. I'm still me. Yeah, I've had to make a little room for this newcomer, but it hardly feels like an imposition.

The Jolly-Rancher got flushed this morning. Along with my sleep. I lean over the sink and spit bile into the porcelain, washing the yellow away. The beginnings of hypoglycemia send shivers over my sweaty skin. I can feel my heart, like *really* feel it. If I rest my fingertips so lightly against the fabric over my chest, I can still feel the ripples of blood pumped out at each interval.

The light feeling didn't go away overnight, but a heaviness has made a paradox in my muscles. Each limb feels like an extra weight previously unaccounted for, heavy and awkward. By the time I stand up and walk to the door, I'm already breathing though my mouth.

Level two privileges mean that I'm allowed phone calls to an approved list of people: my parents. But my dad isn't one worth calling, and I don't know how I could field all my mom's worried questions *and* assure her I'm fine, so I don't call. I do get to go on outings, which are usually movies, but those only happen on the weekends. The gym is still off limits, and so far, I can't see too many advantages to my new status.

On a brighter note, Zena and Emerson have been getting along better. I watch them when I walk around the unit, giggling and teasing each other. I'm always walking, always moving, even in groups. Spikes of anxiety rise up whenever I'm still, so I stick to memorizing every bit of floor in this hospital during those walks.

I've been here 26 days, and still no one dares throw around *discharge* talk. That's 26 days of not sleeping in my own bed. 26 days since I've stepped foot in my own house, or seen my dog, or listened to music, or had even the slightest sense of autonomy. Today, according to Zena, is Hazel's 127th day, which makes me stir crazy just to imagine. Her bowl of alphabet soup (what us psych folks call our lists of diagnoses) is an interesting mixture of self-harm, selective mutism, and PTSD. Or was, since she's being discharged sometime today.

I imagine it'll be pretty quiet, if her departure is in any way related to her reclusive disposition. Still, she was fun to have in art group. Hazel seemed to channel all her words into the same set of four pastels, but her creations were transcendent.

When I get to the common area, Emerson waves me over. Zena is lounging across him, just like the first morning I saw them. "Good morning."

"You mean good afternoon," Emerson teases.

"Hey," I toss a pillow at him, "I'm a psychiatric patient. Sleep is practically a competitive sport."

"Can't argue with that one." Zena stays silent, resting with her eyes closed in agreement.

I turn to Emerson. "Hey, I never asked you. How did your family therapy go?" He blushes and rubs his nose.

"It was…it was brutal. She used her *lawyer* voice on me." He shudders, making me laugh.

Hazel walks airily out of the girls' hallway. She glides up to the nurses' station and says something to Naomi. "Do you know what time she's leaving?"

Emerson follows my gaze and shrugs. "Later in the

afternoon, I think. She's been here over four months, and she still hasn't said more than five words to me."

I play with the hem on my shirt, feeling the anxiety grow the longer I sit. "At least she's better. I can't even imagine being here for so long."

This gathers Zena's interest. "You think Hazel's really better? She barely talks, and she started freaking out in her room the other night." I stare at Zena, and she raises her eyebrows. "Our rooms are next to each other, and they're not exactly soundproof."

We ponder this, all of us watching Hazel write something down for Naomi.

"Does anyone actually get better here?" Emerson and Zena turn back to face me. "It's just, Hazel is still Hazel. Piper hasn't changed much…"

Emerson adds, "And I slipped up. You can add me to that list." Zena's face hardens.

"No. Everyone slips up, it doesn't mean none of us are getting better. Got it?" She stares us both down until we nod. "Good. Now let's lay here and pretend we don't have another eight hours before anything interesting happens today." We fall silent again and rest on the moldy sofa.

With the heat blasting and pine trees, out of every window,

laden with inches of snowy powder, I picture what it must be like for the rest of the world. Fires in hearths, the smell of cinnamon *everywhere,* wreaths on every door. I can feel heat of a mug warming my fingers, see coats strewn around a home, creating an atmosphere of company and togetherness. I can just barely smell the gingerbread cookies my mom bakes every year: clove, nutmeg, and sugar perfuming the kitchen and getting sucked into the vents, carrying the aroma throughout the entire house.

A twinge of sadness disguised as reality snakes through the portrait. Because there is no fire, or family, or cinnamon. Some of the nurses have tried spreading festivity, but there's nothing celebratory about spending the holidays away from family, stuck in a hospital. Yesterday Amanda taped some paper snowflakes to the windows, but the cold has already peeled them from the glass. It's just a reminder of another damn thing we can't have.

We pass the time playing various card games, but you can only spend so many hours with a deck of cards before boredom sets in. Especially if cards were the go-to time killer yesterday, and for the past week, and before that. I thumb though a few pages in one of the books I got with my mom, but my mind keeps sliding away. I end up reading the same page for ten minutes without taking in a single word. The ants in my brain tear up each word I attempt to digest, replacing them with numbers.

Always the same numbers.

I sneak away to my room around five to do a few covert sit-ups. My stomach quivers from the beginning, and even the tops of my legs join in after a while. As always, I keep an eye on the clock, glancing each time I come level to it.

The depression is still, for the most part, at bay, and the relief is palpable. That's not to say I'm filled up on happiness, but the removal of something bad tastes just as sweet as gaining something positive. Even without depression's firm grasp, I still need my fix of exercise. I feel my muscles twitch every time I sit, with every bite of food I swallow. The compulsion to work out is almost as ravenous and insatiable as my hunger.

I pause, five minutes before someone will check on me, and consider doing a few push-ups. My arm is still sore from getting blood drawn earlier, so I skip them. The common area is pretty cleared out when I arrive and plop down into a beanbag. Zena is reading in one of the chairs in front of the TV, and Jeremy is journaling on the art table. I wouldn't be surprised if Hazel already left. The unsaid question, of course, being who will fill in her place. Since admits rarely happen on weekends, I push aside the thought for another day.

It's amazing, this juxtaposition. How yesterday was full of drama and today is drawing on, occupied by a series of activities pursued from boredom. I press my palm against the cold window like some dramatic scene of a movie. My hand drinks in the cold, and my eyes memorize every reflective snowflake glittering the ground. I lean into the cruel window, longing to be just an inch beyond the glass. I'm so close, but so removed at the same time.

So I just watch the snow. I follow birds as they leave tracks in the soft powder. I watch the wind conjure flurries, plowing pileups off branches and from the roof. I can't tell if my ability to stare out a window for three hours is an introvert or a psych patient thing, or maybe they amplify each other, and I'm doomed to stare out windows forever.

Emerson walks sleepily from the boys' hallway and breaks the spell. "Staring contest with a tree?"

I move my eyes to his green ones, flecked with yellow sparks. "The tree won. Movie time? I'm going stir crazy over here."

He chuckles and takes the beanbag opposite me. "Me too. I wish we could go outside more, but then again it's like ten degrees, so maybe not."

"True." I debate asking, but curiosity wins. "Where did you go?" Emerson looks confused for a moment, but it gets wiped away with a grin.

"I never actually made it out of the grounds; this place is a fortress. Eight-foot-high walls all around. I just sort of sat and shivered." He looks away from the memory. "I hope we watch something from this decade. Last weekend Naomi got all nostalgic and made us watch the original *Peter Pan*."

It turns out to be *Patch Adams*, which is definitely not from this decade, and kind of ironic to watch a movie beginning with a psychiatric hospital. Naomi holds open the door to the nutrition room, but I stay seated. Emerson shoots me this sassy look, tipping his head down and raising one eyebrow, grinning like an idiot. I roll my eyes.

He reemerges and plunks down in the seat, holding a cupful of sweets. I guess I'm not the only one who uses that particular method. "Here." Emerson slides something into my hand. Something small, rectangular, and wrapped in plastic.

"I don't like Jolly Ranchers."

He exhales in a laugh. "Yeah, you do. Everyone does. It's ok, Willow. It won't kill you."

I slide the candy into my pocket. The moment I get back to

my room, it's headed for the toilet. Emerson unwraps one of his own and pops it in his mouth. "Mmm. Cherry." I can smell it, wafting every time he breathes out. It should be gross, as a principle of being a girl, but the smell is intoxicating. My heads spins for longing, drunk on the *smell* of sugar. "Drooling is very unbecoming, you know."

"Em, if you don't shut up, I'm going to shove those—!"

"Zena, watch your language." Naomi clicks her tongue and walks over to the nurses' station, her keys jingling into the newly established quiet.

The rest of the movie plays in undisturbed silence, but my eyes keep tracking off the screen. All two hours I can feel the vesicle of sugar in my pocket, warm from pressing on my leg. I *want* to watch the movie. To think about anything else but unorthodox medical students would be a relief. I slip my hand into the pocket and roll it around in my hand.

In what feels like a few short minutes, or possibly several days, the movie ends. I rush off to my room without wishing anyone goodnight and close the door behind me. My heart is sprinting, begging to beat out of my chest. Heat flushes my face and the veins on my hands stand out. Over a Jolly Rancher.

I unwrap it. It's cherry.

I place it between my teeth. Hot air hisses from my nose.

My tongue brushes past it; the synapses in my brain explode.

I close my lips over the end.

The flavor is a drug I can't live without, and I'm greedy. Panic collides with every cell, multiplying in every molecule of euphoria. Fear splits apart the sugar into a poison that tastes like liquid terror. I spit the Jolly Rancher in the trash can and rinse my mouth off in the sink. Tears swirl in the water. My fingers claw around the edges of the basin, grinding into the porcelain with each hiccup. *How could I be so careless? How could I give up control like that?*

Panic works over my body like a puppet master. I cling to the sink, then the bathroom door, but it rips me off the hinges and throws me down on the floor. *No.* I don't want to be on the floor. I want to be in bed, careless, savoring that piece of candy. *I don't want to do this.*

But someone else is calling the shots now. How much damage did those five seconds cause? How much exercise can assuage this blinding panic? My nerves are on fire with it. There isn't enough to reverse the terror; each sit-up should have already happened, too late, too slow, each jumping jack not replaced fast enough by the next. All over five seconds.

All because of Emerson.

Chapter 18

The dull hum of the van lulls me into a trance. I'm squished in the back of a classic, white treatment van, next to Zena. Jeremy sits on her other side. Emerson, with his new rules and restrictions, wasn't allowed to come. I prop one hand up on my cheek and watch grey sludge spin out from the wheels. The freedom to be off the unit, even for a couple hours, sends shivers of delight beneath my many layers.

I turn to Zena, "Do all treatment places have these creeper vans?" She shrugs.

"I don't know. Never been anywhere else. Where have you been?"

I straighten my ponytail and tuck my hands into my jacket. "Just IOP, a few weeks before I came here." IOP is psychiatric jargon for Intensive Outpatient Program. It's like Glenview, but with the bonus of going home at night.

"I didn't know that. I'm betting you have those overly paranoid parents?"

I laugh. "Very perceptive. It was all a waste of time

anyway. You said we're going to a movie theater?"

Zena nods. "Yeah, I'm not sure which movie though. We'll decide when we get there." The fact I never shared that I've been in treatment before makes me wonder what I don't know about Zena. I mean, for people who spend every moment stuck together, there's a lot we don't know. Like the things I didn't know about Emerson. Groups here aren't like in the movies; people don't just spill what deemed them insane, or the very worst things in their lives. Those stay behind closed doors, but I still feel guilty not trying to know either of them better.

The van pulls into a sad strip center with broken glass bottles and lots of potholes. Matt opens the double doors, and we pile out. The frozen air hits my lungs tasting like iron, but I breathe it all in; fresh air is a rare commodity. The other nurse ushers us inside the dimly lit theater and pays for seven tickets to some G-rated movie. A few couples and one family are at the concessions getting snacks. The people keep shooting covert glances at us, like they can somehow smell the crazy.

Thankfully, Naomi and the male nurse are in regular clothes, not scrubs, so our party is at least a degree less conspicuous. "Come on everyone. Move along." We're shepherded down a hall and into a small, dank theater room. They have us sit in the topmost rows, with the two of them in the very first as to get a better view watching us all. Even here, in public, doing real people things, their eyes on the back of my head tie a noose on my sense of freedom. I'm back in kindergarten, unable to even go to the bathroom without asking permission.

I watch the previews and try not to think about my muscles twitching, begging to *move*. Some family a few rows down from us completely breaks all movie theater etiquette. A bratty little kid complains that he's already out of soda. The father swoops in, taking the empty plastic cup, saying, "No problem, buddy. I'll be right back." He stoops low out of the room and disappears. Dad to the rescue. *Enjoy it while you can, kid.*

The movie starts, but I don't really watch it. As if the darkness is a blank screen for my thoughts, I can't stop thinking…about *everything*. About how weird this is to be both a prisoner and out in the world with normal people. Will it always be this way? To feel both here and not here? I remember, even before Glenview, the veil between me and everyone else. Like it's you and depression versus the rest of the world. It cannibalizes every stray, normal moment until it's just you, and it.

Walking through a grocery store means looking at the old lady examining bananas and thinking, *I'm going to die before you.* Or eating cereal and realizing its expiration date is a week after yours. Or saying yes to plans with friends because, what the heck, you're not going to be around for them anyway. Depression is always there, tainting every single facet of life.

Even now, putting up the divide between us and *them*, the kid and his genial dad. I'm like a ghost, able to watch but not be seen. More than a memory, but diaphanous enough to question being really here.

The lights flicker on and credits roll up the screen. I stand up and stretch out my legs, which already feel stiff. Zena shuffles out of the isles and tells me, "Well, that was a waste of two hours. I guess it beats two hours of getting my brain poked with a stick." I laugh, but my head is too full to speak. Naomi and the weekend nurse gather us in the hall and do a head count.

I won't deny how tempting it is, to slip away unnoticed with the tide of people spilling from the theater. Right up until I wander around aimlessly in the dead of winter, or the likely fact of being found and dragged back like Emerson. I lean up against a wall like an obedient patient while someone else makes sure my freedom is nice and caged. "Alright everyone, back to the van. Stay together now." And like well trained dogs, we follow Naomi out. The male nurse marches behind us to catch any strays.

"Back seat again?" I turn to Zena, but she isn't beside me. "Zena?" I break away from the pack and move against the school of bodies. "Zena?" Through a window of shoulders, I spot her tangle of blond hair by the theater doors.

"Hey, where do you think you're going?" The male nurse grabs my arm but when I glare at him, he lets go. I walk over to Zena with the nurse in pursuit and weave through the last stragglers. Before I can reach her, Zena's face makes me freeze in place.

Her eyes are fixed on someone in the mass of dissipating people, and something in them is unhinged. Tears roll down her face, but she seems not to notice them. Her hands are shaking, but the rest of her is statuesque, even her face is frozen, eyes wide, mouth just barely open. "Zena? Are you ok?" She doesn't acknowledge me. Her eyes swivel, following the path of someone moving down the hall. A fresh tear drips down her nose. I walk closer and find that her entire body is shaking. I reach out but let my hand hang in the air. Something is *very* wrong.

"It's him." Her mouth doesn't move when she speaks. Zena's eyes are *scary*, some cross between trepidation and revulsion, and the tears start raining down her face without pause. Something works lose inside her, and she starts forward, shoving people aside, her eyes unblinking and fixed on someone I can't see. The nurse intercepts this and hurries over to Zena. He says something and puts a hand on her shoulder, but the moment he touches her, she flinches and spins away. "Don't. *Touch*. Me." Her words are acid.

"Naomi!" The male nurse yells over heads, and Naomi instructs everyone to wait in the van. Neither one of them seem to notice me, and I stay low to avoid being spotted.

I can *feel* the heat coming off of Zena like she's made of fire. As if we're on the same mental wavelength or channel, I can see the fire unfurl inside her and rise up, ready to burn. "You," she claws into the shoulder of a guy with short, brown hair, "piece of *fucking SCUM!*" He turns around right as Naomi grabs Zena by the arm, hard. The male nurse stands by, waiting to intervene.

Naomi pulls Zena off the guy, and he looks right into her eyes. Comprehension dons his features and he smiles, wide with malice. "Still so beautiful. It's been far too long, Zena. Don't you think?"

Zena snarls at him and the male nurse steps in. "I'm going to tear you to *fucking shreds!*" Together, he and Naomi drag Zena's kicking body out of the building. I follow them, slip unnoticed into the van, and take a look back at the brown-haired guy. His creepy smile exudes delight, watching Zena as she's wrestled into the van.

He steps out through the doors and calls, "Good luck with that, baby. I liked you better when you were sane." The comment sends Zena fighting past Naomi with a savage, wild snarl on her face. Naomi slams the door shut and blocks Zena's exit.

"Naomi, move. You have no idea—he deserves everything—!"

"Zena, look at me. Look at me, right now." The van pulls out of the parking lot, leaving Mr. Creep standing beside the theater with his hands in his coat pockets. All of us keep our heads down and try not to listen, but it's futile. Zena faces Naomi, and their eyes meet. "Deep breaths. In." Naomi inhales. "And out." Her minty breath sends a visible puff of heat into the van.

Zena follows Naomi's lead and takes a few steadying breaths. On the last exhale, she hiccups out a sob and buries her face into Naomi's coat. "It was him, Naomi. It was *him*."

Naomi wraps her arms around Zena and rubs her back. "I know. You're ok, Zena. You're safe with us."

And, I kid you not, we drive all the way back like that. The whole car is struck by an uncomfortable silence as we blaze down the road, just our casual creeper van driving down the highway with a cargo full of crazies. Damaged goods. Zena is clinging to Naomi while all of us stare out windows, trying not to think about whatever horrible crime that man committed. The hum of the van sings the tune of our insanity, and we pull through the gates of a psychiatric hospital. Home.

No matter how many moments of normal we have, the reality is that all of us are incredibly messed up. Normalcy is just a fantasy: a room of one-way mirrors. We have too many hungry skeletons in our closets to pretend that any of us are actually alive.

So we empty out of the van, filing past the series of locked doors, knowing too fully that, for whatever reason, each of us belong here. This is our normal.

Chapter 19

Zena hasn't said anything to us for almost two days. Mondays always seem to form a phalanx of therapy and forced truths, and I hope she can find some peace today. Now it's Emerson's turn to be concerned about the third member of our trio, but I guess these things happen here. All of us try hard, even with each other in our own twisted ways, to provide the fallacy of being sane. But at the end of the day, we all just live together in a building of super concentrated insanity.

At home I never once poked my nose out of line. I did all my homework, never partied, never did drugs or drank. My mom threatened to instill an anti-curfew, saying I came home before any of the fun started. But right now, my stands of rebellion against being held captive are exactly what the doctor ordered.

I work out in my room, not caring if anyone catches me. I come out of my room with a book halfway through Psychotherapy Group and read in the common area. Amanda asks if I'm going to drink the mystery shake, and I tell her no. These may not seem like revolutionary acts, but they are pretty brave (or stupid) since I have no way of outrunning the consequences, which there will be.

The group door opens. Zena is the first to come out, followed closely by Emerson. She sits down next to me and pulls her knees to her chest. Emerson takes the other seat beside her. I look at him, and he shakes his head. I feel so *helpless*. She's right beside me, struggling and trapped in her mind, and I can't do anything to remedy what she's reliving.

"They're making me have some emergency therapy with Dr. Patin. This is the shittiest Monday, I swear."

Her eyes stay fixed on the carpet when Dr. Patin walks out. She walks to the nurses' station and jots something down.

"You're not having it with Webber?" Zena sniffs and wipes at her eyes.

"He's doing intake." Perfect timing, Asylum Gods, well done.

"I forgot. No therapy! But hey, Emerson said Dr. Patin is chill. Right?"

Emerson nods. "Yeah, I did. It'll be ok, *girl*." Zena cracks a tiny smile. "And we are here for you when you get back."

Zena looks between Emerson and Dr. Patin as she approaches.

"What, you mean you aren't leaving me?"

Emerson smiles and rolls his eyes, looking over at the door. "Couldn't if I wanted to, darlin'." He tips an invisible cowboy hat at Zena the moment Dr. Patin reaches us.

She looks me first. Her eyes narrow and she smiles, giving me a *nice try* look. "We missed you in group this morning, Willow."

I stifle a yawn. "Slept in by accident." I feign a frown and elbow Zena through her restrained laughter. "Can't believe I missed my favorite group."

Dr. Patin's smile morphs into amusement. She turns to Zena and claps her hands together. "Well, Zena, are you ready?" She mumbles something that sounds a lot like "God, no" and stands up to follow Dr. Patin. Emerson puts his feet on Zena's cushion and stares at me expectantly.

"It's your turn next," he declares.

"What do you mean?" He scratches at his nose, something he does whenever he gets uncomfortable, and teases out a smile.

"I mean that I had a meltdown, Zena just lost it, so now it's your turn."

I roll my eyes at him. "Well thanks. That's super reassuring."

He laughs and shakes his head. "You know, for two people

living together, I know almost nothing about you." He mimes putting on glasses and peers over them with scrutiny. "Tell me about yourself, Willow."

"Well, *Wilson*, there's not much to tell." His freckles scrunch up into his smile. Emerson, apparently oblivious to basic fashion, is wearing a bright red tee shirt. The cherry color clashes magnificently with his red mane, adding to the ludicrous play acting.

He pushes, "Oh, come on. Let's play twenty questions." I kick out my feet over the top of his.

"You're not going to give up on this, are you?" I watch his fingers link behind his head. The move is so *Emerson* that I give in to a budding smile.

"You astound me with that mind of yours," he responds, squinting at me smugly. How is it there are better friends in a psych hospital than real life?

I shake my head. "You get five. And after you ask a question, I get to ask one about you." He sighs.

"Deal. Complete honesty?" I nod. "When was the first time you cut yourself?" My hands curl in the cuffs of my sleeves. They soak with sweat in seconds.

"Well, dive right in then. You're not going to be like the kids at my last place? They talked about this stuff like it was a competition."

Emerson puts his hand over his heart and says seriously, "Of course not! Who'd want to win something like that anyway?" He thinks for a minute. "That doesn't count as a second question."

I take a deep breath. "It was when I was fifteen, during spring of freshman year. After a track practice." The truth washes over me like ice water. "Your turn. How long have you had bulimia?"

Emerson's smile dissolves and his eyes move over my shoulder, probably staring out the infamous window. "Four years."

My stomach ruptures with anxious butterflies. "Oh my God. You were thirteen? And that's just a clarifying question." His fingers trace over the pattern on the couch, worrying out the truth.

"Yeah. Ed and I are good pals. I didn't know what it was then, though. Have you ever tried to kill yourself?"

It's my turn to look out the window. I hug my arms around my knees and sigh into them, the truth rising into my mouth tasting like bile. "Yes. Have you?"

He answers, "No. But I've thought about it a couple times. What happened?"

I slam my feet into the floor and cross my arms over my chest. "Off limits. Ask something else."

"Ok," he continues cautiously, "what's your favorite color?" I snap my head back to him and raise my eyebrows.

"Well, that was quite the change of subject." A smile splits both out faces. "Blue. Like a dark, midnight blue. What happened with your dad?"

A shadow crosses over his face, setting his features in semi-darkness. "He…wasn't a great father. When I was in middle school, he became abusive. Well, more abusive. When I told you he's not in the picture anymore, it's because he's in jail."

His eyes droop with sadness and I scoot closer, resisting the temptation to give him a hug. "Emerson, I'm *so* sorry. I shouldn't have asked—I didn't know."

He shakes his head and assures me, "It's ok. I'm working on dealing with it." The math isn't hard to add up; Emerson's bulimia emerged in middle school, probably as a way to cope with his dad. He traded one curse for another. "One more question before lunch?"

I agree, "Sure."

He leans back into the grimy armrest and flexes his toes. This can't be good. "Do you want to get better?" The look in his eyes is of deep concern. Emerson isn't asking if I want to get happy and un-depressed; he's asking if I'm going to kill myself.

"Geez, Emerson. Remind me not to play twenty questions with you again." But the comment doesn't make him smile. Emerson looks right into my eyes, unblinking.

Amanda's voice splices the tension clean in half. "Come on, you two! Time for lunch. Emerson, you're back to level one, so you can come with us." Classic to Amanda, she stands over us until we get up and follow her to the door.

Emerson is at my elbow and pleads, "Well?" I open my mouth the same moment Zena rushes over and wriggles her way into the middle of our trio, draping an arm over either of us.

"That was *ridiculous!* Wait until I tell you what that…" The rest of her rant gets swept away by Emerson's huge, begging eyes. I look across Zena and throw him a small smile, but the worry in his eyes intensifies. *Sorry, Emerson, but the truth isn't always easier to swallow.*

Because if I'm sticking to the rules, the answer is no.

I have no intensions of getting better.

The new girl pokes her head out of the hallway leading to Webber's office. She has darker skin and curly black hair, probably of Indian descent, and is trailed by two people in her likeness, her parents. Amanda is standing in wait as the girl says goodbye to her parents.

Both her mother and father give an air of elitist, wealthy people. Her dad is fitted in a suit, and her mother has her hair pulled into a tight bun. She bends at the waist to hug her daughter, but the woman's spine doesn't curve an inch. They both straighten and look around at the unit with upturned noses. As if they can *smell* the crazy. It's clear these people, more than any of our parents, would never, under any foreseeable circumstance, leave their child in a place so lowly.

Anthony escorts them out, and Amanda smiles down at the girl, who looks absolutely terrified. They disappear down the girls' hallway, leaving the rest of us to speculate.

Matt speaks first. "Drugs?"

"Nah," Jeremy counters, "not with parents like that."

Piper offers, "Anxiety?"

Zena scoffs, "No one comes here for *anxiety*. Too boring." In the world of patients, we all rank each other by our most notable offense, like a hierarchy of insanity. The staff rank our cases by most interesting or fascinating, similar to zoo animals. "Well, I guess we can just ask her ourselves." She inclines her head and Amanda brings the shell-shocked girl in our direction. I wonder if she gave her the "making friends is important for your recovery" speech, judging by the clear terror at being guided in our direction.

"Everyone, I want to introduce you to Jordan." Jordan looks around the room, scanning for a place to disappear. She'll soon learn this place is disappear-proof.

Zena is in full girl-mode. "Hi, Jordan! I'm Zena. Come sit, we were just killing some time after lunch. I *love* your shoes, by the way."

"Um, thanks." She takes a seat beside Samson and sits with the straight spine of her mother. We take turns introducing ourselves, by the end of which Jordan has that I-don't-remember-anyone's-name look, which is to say politely mortified. She informs us that she's from Manhattan and is a sophomore, but keeps it strictly demographic.

I do my introvert thing and hang out in the back, taking in more than giving out. I notice how careful all of her mannerisms are: well-practiced smile that doesn't reach her eyes, folded hands, legs crossed at the ankles. She's more mannered than anyone in my high-school, and yet, is locked in a building for *behavioral* health. Of course in this place, the more you try to hide, the more you have to hide.

There's something about her eyes that makes me uneasy.

She's engaged with everyone best she can, but her eyes are also seeing *more*. They flit around the room with purpose, much more intentioned than an absentminded glance. Her shoulders rise and fall faster with each covert scan, but she covers it up by diving deeper into the conversation. Jordan clearly has her own neuroses brewing under that carefully crafted façade, but something seems more off with her.

Amanda comes around the nurses' station with two large suitcases and gestures to Jordan. She excuses herself like a proper socialite and follows Amanda. She'll soon discover the first of many revoked freedoms and comforts, cellphone for starters. Just one of the infinite hazards of psychiatric living.

A brief silence ensues while we watch her walk out of the room. Piper, by nature, is the first to break it. "Shit. I bet her parents are politicians or something. Why is she here?" Piper tucks a loose strand of hair behind her ear and leans in toward us, hungry for gossip.

I interject, "I'm sure she will tell us. There's no need to go poking around; we all know how well that ended up last time." Zena laughs haughtily and flips back a lock of blond hair like someone straight from a high-school popular clique. Emerson even gives me a small smile, inclining his head almost imperceptibly.

Emerson's eyes narrow at something behind me. "Heads up, six o'clock."

I laugh. "This isn't a spy movie!" Turning around, I spot Anthony swaggering over to our group, clipboard in hand.

"Sorry to interrupt. I need to get your vitals, Willow." He gestures to the roll-y chair with the clipboard, and I follow.

Sitting down, I ask, "How much longer do you think I'll have these three-a-day vitals?" I swivel side to side as he untangles the blood pressure cuff. Anthony peels apart the Velcro and wraps the cuff around my arm, refraining from giving an immediate answer. I never noticed before, probably from his propensity for waking me up, but Anthony looks like he got pulled from my cheesy romance novel. Artfully styled hair, lean and muscular, and shaking his head in amusement at my comment.

"For however long you keep up your tirade against food." The cuff deflates, and I stand. "Do you realize what you're doing to your body?"

I sigh. "Oh, not you too. Really, I've gotten this lecture already." The machine whirrs as air is pumped into the sleeve, cutting off the blood flow to my fingers.

"I'm not here to lecture. Just remember, it's you who will

have to live with the consequences." He peels off the cuff and jots down the numbers. I push off the roll-y chair.

"I'll keep that in mind." My feet start down the girls' hallway, leaving Anthony stuck between the pages of his rom-com. The door at the end of the hallway is open, and voices carry out of it.

"Get them off! This place is disgusting!" Jordan's shouts are matched by Amanda's soothing tones. She is saying something, but it's too low to make out. Since my room is two doors before Jordan's, I can't casually peer in to find out what's going on.

A line of ants leads into my room. I follow them, reluctant as I am to acknowledge their infestation. They crawl into the bathroom, marching over the fake mirror and sink. I step in front of the distorted image. Hundreds of black ants run over my reflective eyes, in my ears, peppering my forehead with their multiplying bodies.

They form and reform numbers, the same numbers, until finally my eyes are hollowed into zeros. The ants circle around and around, spiraling in on the unattainable, picking apart every inch of my mirrored face. More climb up from the sink and cover my reflection's mouth, twisting the image so shrewdly it becomes impossible to know what is real. They curl my mouth into a scream.

That scream is the last thing I think about before my palms hit the floor. When I look up, the ants creep under the doorframe and into the hallway. They carry the numbers on their backs, burdened by the heavy load, pleading, demanding to be just a little lighter.

I do another push-up.

And another.

I have to be

just a

little

lighter.

Chapter 20

When I reemerge on Tuesday, back into the same beige common area, with the same beige people, complaining about the *same* problems, I almost walk right back to bed. Instead, Emily, the nutritionist, spots me and waves me over to the craft table. To think I was *so close* to avoiding this makes my limbs feel sandbagged.

Emily, much to my displeasure, is a total morning person. Her shoulder-length auburn hair is flawless and her eyes pop out with excitement. What could make a Tuesday better than finding out exactly how much vitamin A is in a carrot? "Good morning, Willow! Did you sleep well?"

I yawn and take the seat next to her. "Sure. Although I wouldn't turn down a cup of coffee." She shuffles a few papers and smiles. Her teeth are unnaturally white.

"I'm a coffee gal myself. But not everyone's medications mix well with caffeine, so it looks like we'll have to plow right on through the morning." I eye her steaming travel mug, wafting out a suspiciously bitter scent. "But, unfortunately, we're not here to chat about coffee, as much as I would love to.

What I have here are a couple of fact sheets for you to reference, and this week's meal plan." She shuffles the papers until she picks out one with a lot of empty boxes.

Planning every meal and snack for the next seven days is practically the opposite of how I planned to "plow through" the morning. I nod toward the other papers and ask, "What are those references for?"

Emily pulls the other two out and lays them side-by-side. "This one here is a diagram of how water functions in the body, and exactly why it's important to stay hydrated. And this," she slides another paper on top, "is a list of some of the important nutrients and vitamins we need from food, and how they support the body." The paper is packed with writing from top to bottom, and I'm not sure it's even written in English. My eyes find "hematopoietic" and "niacin". Definitely not English.

"Looks fascinating. I was thinking…is a meal plan really necessary? Because I don't know what the cafeteria is always serving that day, and sometimes the foods I'm supposed to eat don't seem that appealing at that time." Emily gives me a knowing look but keeps smiling. She pulls out the empty meal plan and sets it on top.

"The benefit of a meal plan is to make sure that you are giving your body everything needs from foods. Before coming here, what did your diet look like?" In all honesty, most of that time is covered in black memory fog, so I can't be entirely sure. I decide on my more recent diet.

"Um, I eat fruit. Carrots. Stuff like that." The medical-laden fact sheet comes soaring back to the top.

"See here," she points out, "you don't get enough of certain nutrients from fruit and vegetables alone. Protein, for instance, isn't found in high amounts in these food groups."

I return the smile, but my eyes flick to Emerson and Zena, and in the corner beanbag, Jordan. All I need to do is placate her and then I'll be free to do…well…nothing. "Right. Well, that makes more sense. I'm not that picky, so I'm fine with whatever meals are best."

While this seems to multiply her indecent amount of morning cheerfulness, planning the week does not go any faster. After ten minutes we only make it to Sunday, and I suggest a few repeat meals to hurry the process. Emily finally seems satisfied after the chart is filled out and checks it one last time.

"I'm going to go make a copy of this, but those two are yours to keep." I nod. She ambles off behind the nurses' station and busies herself at the copier. Gathering the papers, I make my way slowly to my favorite crazy people and smoosh down between them.

Emerson pokes me in the arm and jokes, "That looked like fun. Meal planning?" I nod, and our couch relaxes into the quiet. The routine of being here is so ingrained that the insane parts—being locked in a building, having zero say in what happens to me, and forfeiting every ounce of personal agency—feel frighteningly commonplace. I don't know what it is, maybe the word "hospital", but I kind of thought that by now, the people here would at least be a little saner than when we first met. "Hospital" implies both sickness and a cure, but none of us are cured.

I think about Samson with his parents who try to live through him, Emerson with the mother of all dad problems, or even Zena who also fell victim to circumstance. The only "cure" being dished out here are the lessons on how to deal with the cards we've been dealt, and that isn't changing a damn thing for anyone. At least not on the outside.

"Willow. Anyone in there?" Emerson's voice interrupts my cyclical parade of pessimism.

"What is it?" He leans back and points to the whiteboard across from us.

"Have you checked the whiteboard?" I shake my head. "You have therapy with Webber in like three minutes." I sigh and let my head fall into a pillow, squishing out all the air.

I moan, "No, I didn't. I just was kind of hoping he'd forget about rescheduling. What do you think will happen if I pretend I didn't know?"

Zena laughs, but Emerson is the first to recover. He looks up at the ceiling and says truthfully, "I think they would know that you were lying. And besides, you already missed group this morning. They might get worried…" The threat makes my palm sweat, because worrying the staff is signing away the small fortunes I still have.

"You're right, but don't get too smug about it. Ok, well then, wish me luck." Emerson nods an invisible hat, and Zena waves goodbye through a yawn. I pad down the hallway and, to punctuate the morning, find his door open.

"Come on in." Instead of finishing a note or scanning over a file, Webber is sitting straight with his hands clasped in front of him. Not that arriving to this office ever gave me waves of excitement, but the atmosphere feels starkly different today. I've seen that look before, in my Mom's eyes, in the eyes of my old IOP therapist. That's the *intervention* look. "Have a seat, Willow."

I close the door and sit down on the leather chair. Today it feels cold and stiff and not at all too-comfortable. His office, usually warm and inviting, is cold as the winter landscape outside the window. I thought things were going *better*; I thought they saw progress, not regression. My exercising has been careful; I've managed my way around meals and stuffing my face. This shouldn't be happening. Maybe he's bluffing? Can shrinks do that?

Webber's intense character doesn't break. His eye contact elicits blinding panic, unearthing the urge to *run*. He prods, "How have you been?"

I meet his stare directly, trying my hardest to convey sincerity and confidence. "I've been fine." My eyes shift down to my toes, then out the window, then just over his shoulder; anywhere but that stare.

"Willow," Webber presses, "how have you really been?"

"I've been fine, like I said," I snap back. I focus my body language to patching up any leaks. Flat mouth, neutral. Fidgety hands, anxious, but natural. It's a delicate balance; too nervous and I'm busted, but too calm and I'm focusing too much on the lie.

My sharp tone just glances off him. "What does fine mean?"

I measure my breathing before speaking. "Fine means fine. There isn't always a secret meaning behind what I say. Sometimes a cigar is just a cigar," I counter, deliberately quoting Freud.

Webber sighs quietly. "Willow, I've heard that you haven't been fine. There are people, including myself, who are concerned." My eyes narrow at the leafless tree. Cool, level anger builds up inside. I feel both detached and ready to strike. "What are you thinking right now?"

I float on sweet currents of *direction* and leave words behind. I'm done with this. I'm done with these questions, with Webber, with no one ever telling me what the hell is going on in my own treatment. I'm *done,* done with this life of mine everyone else is trying to preserve. I'll call my mom, tell her what's going on, lie. She'll bring me home. She has to.

I wipe my palms on my pants. With a last look at Webber, I stand up and walk to the door. "Willow," Webber calls, "if you don't talk to me, we are going to have to revoke your level two privileges."

Depression-anger, finally returned, licks up like fire against my skin. The kind of unique anger that says screw the consequences; it doesn't matter anymore. Nothing *matters*. In the silence, I hear my heart beating vehemently. My voice doesn't come out as a shout, but I spit the words at him. "What? *What* do you want me to say?" His eyes stay fixed on mine, but Webber stays silent. "Is there a problem with being fine? Do I need to come in here falling apart and completely broken for it to be ok? If that's the case, then there's no reason for me to be here. None at all."

My chest is rising and falling, ready to launch more words at Webber. And *Webber* just sits in his chair, rolling the stupid pen. He at least has the decency to frown, but his face shows not a flicker of alarm. If he says something preprogrammed like, "Willow, you seem upset", I'm out of here. He breaths out another quiet sigh. "Why do you think you're here?"

He is seriously determined; I'll give him that. My hand is on the doorknob, but I want to finish this. I smile and shake my head. "Why don't you tell me? From where I'm standing, there isn't a single reason why I need to be here. I have never done anything to warrant this. To be trapped in this 'hospital' against my will, *indefinitely*. There isn't. A *single*. Reason."

I shouldn't be here.

I shouldn't be here.

I shouldn't be anywhere but underground, and that's the only place I plan on leaving to.

Webber has that posture of someone trying so hard to hold it together. I can see how badly he wants to diffuse this and how afraid he is to cut the wrong wire. Good. I'm tired of being the only one on edge. I twist the knob and pull open the door. Without looking over my shoulder, I tell him, "Why don't you *give it some thought*," and shut the door behind me.

I feel fueled with emotion, revved up and alive. This mixture of depression's return, pain and an overflow of emotion, and the last dregs of anger are like an emotion high. I stride down the hallway before Webber does or doesn't do whatever comes next.

When I get to the common area, I pause. I've never wanted to be home so badly as I do now. I picture myself walking out into the snow, coatless, into the woods. I want to walk and walk and walk until the cold starts to *hurt* then bathe in it. I want to feel frozen steel under my fingertips, bringing my intrinsic deadness to fruition.

But I can't do anything here. And even though I don't feel hungry anymore, I want to eat everything in the nutrition room until I'm drunk with sugar. Or I want to exercise until I pass out. One thing is clear: I have to do *something*.

When I get to my room, there are no ants. I curl my hands into fists and bang them against the window, quiet enough not to draw attention. The emptiness, the lightness, has popped like a balloon, sending me plummeting into Earth.

My thoughts are racing at a speed I haven't felt in a long time, and I almost feel dizzy with their pace. I want to get out of here right now I *have* to get out of here I can't do this I don't want to feel this anymore I want this to end please *justmakeitend*. Outside the window, everything is white. Pure, untouched whiteness. The black thing inside wants to ruin the flawless powder. I want to stain it grey like it was *that* night, under the obsidian sky speckled with dying stars. I want to Windex the smudge in my memory and find out what happens next.

There's a knock on my door, and I straighten up. "Willow? Are you doing alright?" Anthony takes a couple steps into the room and looks me over. He has his hands in his pockets and pulls his eyebrows up with concern. What I really need right now is privacy.

"Doing great. Thanks." I walk over to my desk and pretend to look for something while Anthony stands there. Not leaving. "Really, I'm fine."

He shrugs, but his face is still full of worry. "Ok, I'll leave to implode in privacy. You looked pretty upset coming out of Dr. Webber's office, but if you change your mind, you know where to find me." Thank God it's Anthony. He's the closest thing to human in this place.

I give a tight smile. "Thanks." He nods and walks out but widens the door all the way open, a subtle warning. I hurry into the bathroom and shut the door. There isn't as much room to pace and freak out, so it all gets compressed, the pressure squeezing in until it's fit to burst.

I collapse in the shower. A few water droplets hug the floor, but the tile is mercifully dry. Tears spill from my eyes like they can't escape fast enough. I'm breathing too fast, and the room starts to spin. I bang my head again and again into the wall.

Ugly. Fat. This will never end. Oh my god this will never end. I can't take this anymore.

My entire body is overflowing with emotion, trying so hard to get *out,* but it still isn't fast enough. I screw up my eyes to try and block out the pain but to no avail. A surge of depression-pain sends my face tipping skyward and my mouth wide with a silent scream. I lace my fingers into my hair and curl them tight around the roots, sobbing silently on the floor of a psychiatric hospital bathroom, personifying the stereotype of a who I really am.

But the pain is relentless. I fall sideways on the floor

and gasp wildly for the air filling everything but my lungs. Black spots take up residence in my vision, and I sob through all the pain. Without thinking, I plunge my fingers into my legs and dig.

The pain isn't immediate, but my hands act of their own accord. They scrabble through layers of skin mining for a source of relief. *Anything*. I feel the skin peeling away, but my fingers keep going, keep digging, trying to find the off switch to this pain.

There. Right *there*, the skin most medial on my leg. Physical pain rushes through every cell of my body like a raging sea, extinguishing every smoldering particle inside me. The relief sends fresh tears pouring down my face. I push myself back up to a sitting position, tip my head back, and sigh with pleasure. With sweet, sweet relief.

I sit like this for a minute, not wanting to assess the damage. There isn't anything enjoyable about this: the concealing clothes, the lies, the excuses, or the physical damage. There's nothing glamorous about being addicted to self-harm, especially when it's just a means of survival. But in the expanse of relief, I actually laugh. Because nothing matters except that the pain is gone.

For this beautiful moment, it doesn't matter that

depression is back, that the pain might not ever really leave, or that it could get worse. All that matters right now is the riptide of endorphins, pulling me out to a sea of bliss.

I think I've been laying here for a while. My toes are pins and needles. With a steadying breath, I take a look at my leg. The affected area is about the diameter of a tennis ball, and not very pretty. After all this practice, my hands are deft with crafting and applying bandages. As I wrap it up, I wonder, my post self-harm ritual, about the consequences. I'll have to alter my gait to pull off walking normally. Tonight will be a sleepless night spent on my back unless I want to painfully bump the wound or dislodge the bandage, which is constructed of no actual medical supplies.

Despite the inevitable itching, the new scar, the possibility of infection, I'm finally empty again. I clean up the bathroom and flush anything incriminating. Before I leave the room, I take a couple moments to smooth over my complexion. I look down and make sure that the bandage isn't visibly bulging, and that I'm overall presentable to a room full of body language hawks.

As I walk down the hallway, I run my hand along the wall, ebbing away my nerves with the cold touch. The common area is emptied except for Jordan eating lunch in the nutrition room.

She's the only level zero here, unless Webber followed through on his threat? Anthony waves me over to the nutrition room. "Here," he says, "I thought I'd let you cool off before lunch. They sent you up a tray." He gestures to the seat next to Jordan where indeed a tray is waiting.

I curl my sleeves into my hands. "That was nice, I'm just not feeling food right now." I look away from Anthony's scornful stare to the pile of food. There's a mountain of ravioli, an apple, orange juice, a replacement shake, and an energy bar. Hopefully they were just aiming for selection, because imaging anyone eating all of that makes me sick.

But you have eaten that. More than that! My palms start to sweat. Anthony props his elbow on the table and leans his head into his hand. He suggests, "It's your choice, but have a seat anyway. Jordan was just telling me about horseback riding." He nods toward the chair, and I reluctantly accept it.

The ravioli sauce wafts into my nose, making my mouth water. I play and rewind the image of biting into a crisp apple. The food doesn't make me hungry; hunger cues are a thing of the past. It makes me *obsessed*. My stomach feels full, but, although I would deny it if anyone asked, it takes all I can to keep myself from stuffing it all down in one sitting. I lean back in the chair, away from the food. It's just an urge, something I can master.

Anthony would never be so outright, but he wants me to sit here in front of the food the same way Emerson left the Jolly Rancher on my bed. I steel myself and pull my thoughts from the vapors. "I've never been horseback riding. Do you ride for a company?"

Jordan flicks a couple peas into a pile of mashed potatoes, then aims a few carrot bits into the ravioli pile. "I used to," she starts, "but now I just help out." Her eyes watch the peas slowly become swallowed into the mashed potatoes with an intensity I'm too familiar with. The nice thing to do would be to let her have space, but I'm nosy, and this place makes us hungry for secrets.

"It always looked really fun. I have a friend who competes, and the way she describes it sounds amazing." A lie, but am I too obvious? My subtleties lie with body language, not *actual* language.

Jordan flattens her mashed potatoes, sending the peas running into the ravioli. She supplies, "Yeah, it can be fun. It didn't work out for me, but I hope your friend enjoys it." Anthony doesn't say anything, and I let the pause stretch. Maybe she'll fill it in? Jordan takes a cautious drink of water, like she's afraid it's contaminated. "I guess all of us have things we had to give up," Jordan concludes.

Very true, and very evasive. I like her. The distant sounds of chatter get louder with everyone returning from lunch. Anthony looks at both of our uneaten plates and asks, "Are you guys done?" With a cohesive nod, Jordan and I find good seats in the common area right as everyone comes flooding in.

"Willow!" Emerson waves over Samson's tall frame. "Are you boycotting the cafeteria now?" His easy smile and casual banter fill my empty stomach with guilt.

I tell him, "Nope. Just a post-therapy nap." He laughs and pulls Zena onto the couch. I honestly can't remember having had better friends, sane or not. Zena and Emerson flow with each other like the friendship is as easy as anything. She pokes him in the arm, and he shoves a pillow between them like a concrete barrier, gesturing to the invisible divide. Zena takes the pillow and smacks him in the face.

Emerson winces. "I get that." A wildly mad grin spreads across his face, making him look indecently happy for someone who recently got a reset button on his treatment.

I incline my head to him and parrot, "You know if you keep doing that, your face will get stuck. What is it?" He rubs his freckled nose and gives a short laugh. Zena looks at him curiously.

"Well, Zena had a royal freak-out this weekend, we had an admit yesterday, you look one wasted replacement shake away from passing out, and I just got bumped up to peeing with the door shut. What a life, Willow."

This isn't the movie where boy meets girl; girl is broken, but boy's love saves her, and they live happily ever after. This isn't even the movie where a tight bunch of friends band together and save each other. We may all be friends, but all of us, at the end of the day, are alone in our own heads. We're all in the same jail, but trapped in our own cells. What a life it is indeed.

Chapter 21

I've dreaded this all day yesterday. Thursday. Family therapy with Webber. Like I said, there isn't any outrunning the consequences in this place, and I don't know what is going to happen. Webber didn't drop my level, but I don't expect Tuesday to just breeze past undiscussed.

I can't even face Emerson or Zena before therapy. Their encouragement would only add anxiety, and I'm trying to put a lid on my nervousness before Webber can dissect it. Which gives me all of five minutes. I stand up and walk to the window, grimacing at the pain in my leg. The wound has scabbed over for the most part, but now its red and sore. Other kids here have self-harmed, but they've all been caught, which means revocation of privileges and your own personal staff to follow you everywhere, not to mention extending your stay.

But I'm two for two so far, and I'd like to keep it that way. I walk around some more, letting the pain chip away at my anxiety until my nightstand clock tells me I have to leave. I walk quickly down the hall and past the common area, breathing easier with every sore step. When I get to Webber's office, the atmosphere feels as thick as it did on Tuesday. I swallow and take a seat.

Webber says hello louder than normal, and I notice that he already has my mom on speaker phone. This is a first. Her voice echoes through the office. "Hi, honey." Her words sound tight and forced. She doesn't ask the myriad of mom-questions, which sends up a major red flag.

"Hi, Mom. How have you been?" Out of the corner of my eye, I watch Webber fold his hands and look down at his notepad. Already filled.

"Oh, I'm alright. Worried, of course." Is it too late to hightail it out of the office? My instincts scream of something ominous and foreboding.

Webber leans forward. "Willow, I was thinking we could jump right into this session. Both of your parents are worried with what we like to call a 'plateau' in treatment, and one of the biggest challenges of dealing with mental illness in families is lack of understanding. To help them out, could you explain to your mom what your experience with depression feels like?"

I look out the window, wishing I could bury myself under all the snow. A deadness fills my chest, pulling my eyes deeper and deeper outside, farther and farther into nothingness. What does *this* feel like?

It's a fatigue that goes deeper than my bones, into the very core of my being. It's a pain that supersedes anything fathomable, without the promise of ever ending. I remember walking outside without a jacket when it was 20 degrees and snowing, yet not feeling cold. It's like the chord struck inside you is finally in resonance. As if someone painted a landscape of your emotions and you walked right into it, a raw, stinging cold and endless snow. It's finally reaching equilibrium with the thing inside you by being somewhere cold and dark.

It's being in a body too lethargic to keep itself warm, and still never being able to sleep. I know my mom doesn't understand, because if she did, I wouldn't need to be in this place. Because there is only one way someone recovers from this.

In all of my reminiscing, probably three seconds have passed. I keep my eyes on the window and say, "It's the same thing you read about on the internet. Being lazy and mopey, but as a lifestyle."

My mom speaks up before Webber. "I read an article the other day about depression. It said that part of the problem is thinking negative. Thinking positively and practicing gratitude are supposed to really help with depression."

I know she means well, but really? I argue, "Mom, if being positive and thinking happy thoughts could cure depression, you think I would have tried that by now."

Webber cuts in, "Those are both helpful ways to alleviate certain depressive symptoms, but like all mental health challenges, depression is a complex illness, and requires a multitude of treatments and therapies."

I think my mom says something to remedy her part, but my thoughts carry me out of the room, into the snow. She and Webber chat back and forth for a few minutes, clearing up stereotypes and finding out the best ways to push me past this plateau, but I'm far away from the office. If my mom wasn't on the other line, I would be physically, too.

The lack of static snaps my thoughts back into the office. Webber leans back into the chair and surveys me. "Well that was quick."

"Willow, we need to talk about what's going on. We don't have to talk about Tuesday if you open up with me about what's been happening." This week was headed downhill before it began, and I don't see a foreseeable end thanks to Webber.

I shrug. "Maybe it has something to do with being here

when I shouldn't be." My palms sweat.

He presses, "What changed? You were making progress, and the fact that you are here isn't any different."

I meet his eyes, determined to end this conversation before it can start. "Nothing has changed. I don't know what you're referencing, but you aren't working with the entire picture. Look, I'm sorry if I've been sending the wrong signals, and that my parents are concerned, but I'm really ok." I tip my eyebrows up in sincerity, but Webber doesn't swallow the lie. It's worked plenty of times. Either he's too good at his job, or he's conditioned not to trust patients insisting on being healthy.

His eyes flick to the clock and back to mine almost imperceptibly. Webber rolls the pen between his fingers in a gesture of defeat. "If you want to lie to me, I don't mind. You are only hindering yourself. We can be done for today, but from now on, I would like you to check in with staff once a shift." He caps the pen and continues, "You should know, at the rate your health is declining, medical intervention might be necessary in the future."

I nod and leap from the chair. My therapist in IOP used to bluff about things to try and make me open up, like *you can talk to me now, or you can talk to someone else at the hospital.* I called her bluff, and all was fine. But everything I've gathered about Webber says he's more straightforward than that. Probably to get honesty in return.

I try to slip back to my room unnoticed, but Amanda calls me over for vitals. She's mercifully un-patronizing, merely telling me when I can stand and when I can go. I spot Emerson on a lone couch, but Zena is nowhere to be seen. Emerson smiles when he sees me and asks, "Going to join us for shame group, or do you need another post-therapy nap?"

"As tempting as *shame group* sounds," I say, "I think I'll pass."

Emerson sits up to make room for me. I squish down and cross my ankles, waiting for the lecture. But he just teases, "And miss the chance for Tyler to infect you with his hipster ways? That's hashtag heartless." I laugh and close my eyes, imagining that a simple group boycott will earn me an hour to myself. "I can always steal his beanie for you. Five starbursts say he'll wear it today."

I shake my head. "No contest. But I'll need his square-framed glasses to really pull off the look."

Emerson puts his hand over his heart, mocking offense. "I think you greatly overestimate my thieving skills, milady." Tyler walks through the unit doors, sporting a grey button-down, dark-wash jeans, and a forest green beanie. "But if it is what you desire…"

    Tyler and Megan drop their stuff off at the nurses' station and stride into the room. "Group time, everyone," Tyler announces. "Don't forget to grab you sheets from last week." Emerson gives the obligatory moan and sits up slowly.

    "You are seriously lucky. He never looks that cheerful unless it means major mind invasion."

    He walks into the group room, and I call after, "Enjoy!" Zena comes walking out of the girls' hallway looking fresh, as usual, and smiles at me before disappearing into group.

    I stand up and walk to the girl's hallway, but a passing Tyler stops me. "Aren't you joining us?" I smile and shake my head.

    "I'm not feeling the best, sorry."

    He nods. "Well, you should probably talk to a nurse. We can't have you missing the best group!"

    "Very true." I walk toward the nurses' station in the direction of Amanda. She straightens up when she sees me approach her and walks around the desk.

    "Is there something you need?"

    "I just need a phone to call my mom." I shove my hands into my hoodie pockets. She looks toward the group room and back to me.

"Why aren't you in group?"

I sigh. "I want to call my mom. The timing isn't ideal, but this time at home she has her lunch break." Should I be frightened with how easily lies come now? Things I've learned since arriving at Glenview include how to lie, hide, and scheme. Quality life skills.

"I'm sorry, Willow, but your phone privileges have been revoked." She crosses her arms like I'm being deliberately annoying.

"But," I protest, "I thought I was on level two?"

Amanda nods. "You are, but you don't have phone privileges at the moment."

I smile and say, "Right. Well, thanks."

My feet start toward my room, but Amanda's comment lassos me. "If you aren't going to group, then you need to stay in the common area." Where she can spy on me. I march back to the couch and sit with my back to Amanda. This sudden loss of phone privileges smells suspiciously of Webber. But *why?* Isn't communicating with my parents supposed to be a good thing, something to be encouraged?

Unless he didn't want me talking to them. If he wanted to punish me, he would choose something that didn't impose on my therapy. Which means he *didn't* want me talking to them. To prevent them from telling me something, or prevent me from begging them to take me home? Either way, it's an unsettling development.

Chapter 22

The crackle of the walkie-talkie makes me jump from sleep. I roll over groggily to the nightstand and grab the speaker. "Willow!" Zena's shrill tones do not pair well with morning, especially a *Saturday* morning.

"What?" My voice comes out a little snippy.

"I wouldn't have woken you if it wasn't a totally big deal." The line goes dead, and I sit up, rubbing away the last remnants of sleep from my eyes. "You'll never believe what Nurse Uptight is letting us do for the outing. We're going *sledding*!" I half expected Zena to stay back this outing, given last weekend, but the excitement in her voice would argue otherwise.

My feet hit the floor, and I drag my tired legs into the bathroom. The moment I step onto the tile, a wave of lightheadedness sends me grasping at the sink. Nausea rolls threateningly in my stomach, and the tips of my fingers start tingling. I turn on the tap and run my hands under the cool water. The feeling helps straighten my spinning head, but the pins and needles feeling remains a few moments longer.

But Zena's excitement is infectious, and by the time I straighten out my vision and head to the common area, I feel more awake than ever. The room is filled with patients and nurses and a mound of coats and gloves. The moment after I spot that signature red mane, a pair of gloves comes flying in my direction. "Incoming!" Emerson laughs as the gloves smack me in the face.

"Well, good morning to you too," I snipe back. I pick out an old, puffy, colorful jacket that looks like it's straight from the 70's and a fresh-smelling hat. With everyone's combined enthusiasm for today's outing, it takes less than ten minutes to get dressed and stand begging at the door. Like happy dogs, at least.

Naomi presides over us and does a head count with another nurse, whose name I should probably know by now. "Alright everyone, it's a bit of a drive, so if anyone has to go to the bathroom, they should do it now." No one moves. The other nurse unlocks the door and herds us all into the van.

Emerson, Zena, and I pile in the back seat. With all of our extra gear, it's quite a tight fit, and I get squeezed into the window. "I am *so* excited, guys. I haven't been sledding since I was like 12. I hope we go to Copper Ridge! That's where my parents used to take us." Zena gets a dreamy, faraway look while she speaks, and casts her gaze out the window.

For about twenty minutes, we sit in silence as the snow gets deeper and deeper outside. Our bodies move and sway together with each bump and turn, a kind of silent dance. The heat in the van has finally kicks in, sending blasts of dry, hot air into the cramped car. I lean my head against the window and drink in the cold, but heat still snakes its way under my nostrils, cooking me from the inside.

"Alright everyone, this is it," Naomi calls from the front. She pulls the van into a partially snow-cleared parking lot, and the vents die with one last shuddering gust. Jeremy opens the double doors, and cold whooshes into the cabin. It must be 15 or 20 degrees, but the cold feels *good*, almost intoxicating. Any sleepy remnants the heat poured into my muscles are sliced apart by the biting breeze outside.

I breathe it in until my lungs hurt and I taste copper, but I'm greedy for how alive and alert the cold feels. The dizziness I felt this morning still lingers, but for now all that matters is how tempting the foot of packed snow looks on that hillside.

Naomi and the other nurse pull old, plastic sleds from the

top and back of the van. "We don't have enough for everyone, so some of you might have to partner up." Emerson, Zena, and I exchange looks and take the longest, least cracked, purple sled.

Emerson shouts, "I'm driving!" and marches up the slippery hill. Zena and I follow behind him, placing out feet in his footsteps. There are mostly younger kids with families, but a few look our age. They exchange curious glances with one another as our party, minus Naomi and her sidekick, parade up the hill, like an army of brightly colored marshmallows. *Criminally insan*e marshmallows.

Each step feels awkward and restrained from the bulky clothing, and by the time I reach the top, I'm panting and lightheaded. "Alright," Emerson commands, "I'll be in front, and the back person will have to push us off and jump in before we get too far." He positions the sled at the crest of the hill while Zena and I exchange glances.

I shake my head and laugh, "I guess I'll do it, but if we run into a tree, you get all the credit, Emerson."

He slides into the front and awkwardly folds in his legs. "Deal." Zena shuffles in behind him, and her toes just barely hang over each side of the cheap, completely unsteer-able purple sled. "We're ready when you are, Willow."

I take a deep breath and heave the sled forward.

Immediately it tips down the hill, gaining momentum of its own accord. My fingers, even through the gloves, dig into the ridge of plastic, and I vault myself in just as Emerson starts whooping.

The sled is so thin, each ridge of ice and pocket of snow pokes at us with unsettling lurches. We bump along the flattened, icy trail of some predecessor. It's clear that Emerson, in all his enthusiasm, has no control over where we go. There's a loop of rope around the front he pulls like reins, but the sled plows onward, completely undeterred.

As we zoom down the hill, our sled starts pulling left. "Emerson!" I shout at him. "Let's avoid the trees!" But "trees" acts like a trigger word, and our untamed sled cuts a path right for a small grove.

Zena yells over all the grinding, "We need to bail!"

"When?"

"Now!" The three of us roll to the right, and our death-sled barrels head-on into the trunk of a pine. The three of us land in a large pile of shoveled-off snow, and it takes incredible effort to work free. When we are finally un-banked, the three of us exchange glances and burst with laughter. Emerson has large chunks of snow in his hair, making him look like a very angry leprechaun, and somehow Zena looks completely untouched except for a flyaway hair escaped from her hat.

Zena punches Emerson in the arm, and he falls back into the mound of snow. "You are never driving again, Em." Emerson chuckles and throws his hands up in surrender. I walk gingerly toward the sled and examine the damage. For the force it had, there's only a tiny crack on the front.

"Well, if either of you wanted to nearly die again, it looks pretty ok." I pass the sled to Zena, and she takes a look at the front.

"You know what, I just might. But we should trade with Jeremy first, to avoid the almost-dying part." The two of them start back up the hill, but I lean my hand against a tree. Heat creeps up my neck with a surge of nausea.

Emerson turns around and sees me before I can compose myself. He asks nervously, "You good, Willow?"

I smile. "Yeah! You guys go ahead. I'm just going to grab some water." He looks at me for a few more moments, and my smile starts to wane. Finally, Emerson nods and jogs to catch up with Zena.

Each step I take toward the van, blood whooshes in my ears, and the ground teeters precariously. I take deep breaths in through my mouth, but the nausea keeps climbing. Five steps from the van, I hunch over and heave bile. Despite being in the cold, my body is flushed with a sickly heat. I watch the snow stain yellow.

"Willow? Are you alright?" Naomi hurries over to me with wild concern in her eyes. Holding my stomach, I straighten up and manage a smile.

"Yeah," I say weakly, "I'm fi—"

"Willow?"

The yellow slides sideways, up the mountain, into the sky. Cold trickles into my ears and I heave again, but I can't find the ground. Everything is spinning and hot and I'm shaking. There's something sticky on my face and someone is yelling and everything is white.

My legs are raised, and the spinning slows down. "There you are, Willow. You're alright. Just lay still." Naomi's voice is composed and soothing with a hint of controlled urgency. She turns to someone else. "Call Jody. Tell her we're coming back early." She sets my feet down and leans over me. Her brown curls swing down around her face, and she wraps her fingers around the pulse in my wrist. "How do you feel?"

"Better. I'm fine. Really." I sit up, but she grabs my elbow when I try to stand.

"Take it easy." She pulls open the van doors and guides me inside. "Sit in the front row. I'll be right back." Naomi hurries over to the male nurse and points to the sled hill. He nods and walks away in the same urgent strides.

I push off the seat and climb out of the van right as Naomi turns back in my direction. "I don't think so," she bosses. "Get back in the van."

I throw my hands up. "I feel fine! Seriously, this is ridiculous." I peel off my gloves and walk defiantly to the hill. Naomi blocks my path and links her arm in mine. I try to wriggle free, but she just grips on harder.

She looks me directly in the eyes with a sternness akin to my mom. "Willow, this is serious. We're all going back to the unit, and you're going to have to start talking when we get back."

I slide back into the van, and she gives me a last hard look before closing the doors. In the quiet, I can hear my breathing, fast and hard. My mouth still tastes like puke, and my lips are starting to go numb. *I'm fine. I'm fine. I'm fine.*

Out of the window, I watch our party of defeated-looking marshmallows finish their last runs and walk solemnly toward the van. My heart thrums with anxiety because despite the *I'm fine*'s in my head, I'm definitely not fine.

I don't think I've been fine for a while.

I stare at Dr. Wilson from across the treatment team room—the same one I was brought to for that "intervention" talk. Yesterday, when we got back, Naomi called an internal medicine doctor, who did a five-minute exam and made a note to call Dr. Wilson.

So here we are. According to the schedule, this meeting is back to back with therapy with Webber. I watch Dr. Wilson flip through a file—my file—as his eyebrows pull closer with each turn of the page. He sighs and straightens his glasses before meeting my eyes. I resist the urge to look away and smooth my palms against my pants, wiping away the sweat.

"How do you feel?" The intensity of his stare raises goosebumps. There's a knowing and a finality behind his eyes that replaces my fear with dread. When you *know* something bad is coming, more than you fear its possibility.

"I feel fine." I float the lie out into the room not to fool Dr. Wilson, because that was never in the cards, but to demonstrate that I'm done with this. I never realized the depression was back because it came so insidiously in the night. But now that it is, I have no energy to fight it anymore. I lean back into the seat, into that resolute doneness, and meet his gaze. *There's nothing left to see through.* I can feel how slack my face is, cold and still, like a corpse.

He doesn't move an inch, not to adjust his posture or straighten his glasses. "You certainly don't look fine." I don't care anymore. Because the sooner he realizes that after all this time, nothing has changed, I'll go home. "What happened on Sunday?"

"I was dehydrated. Naomi made sure I drank water when we got back. I feel fine now."

"Willow, we both know this is more than dehydration. Your labs still haven't improved from the last time we spoke." He taps a finger on the file. "I told you that if this was the case, you would be placed on room and bathroom restriction. I'm sorry, but if your health doesn't start improving in the next 48 hours, that is to say staff see you eating according to your meal plan, then medical intervention will be necessary."

His stare is piercing, giving off the usual feeling of being examined like my thoughts are transparent. Beneath the scrutiny is a kindness, like if I just opened up, he could put my thoughts and emotions back in order and I would be shipped off, a girl of reassembled parts. But the people who are best at spotting lies make the best liars themselves.

This doneness is a puppeteer for my actions. It pulls the strings and I nod my head, pinch my eyes in a fake smile. I don't know what expects me to say, but he doesn't speak. Does he think I'll argue and try to make a case for myself? That would be entering a world of false hope where inevitably, I lose. There's nothing I can say to change what's about to happen, not matter how much I will it not to.

"What are you thinking about?"

I bring my lips to match the false warmth in my eyes. "Nothing. Is that everything you wanted to talk about?" Dr. Wilson tilts his head to the side, trying to get a better read, and squints through his glasses.

"Willow, what's going through your mind?"

I sigh and glance to the door. "Please don't answer my question with a question. I don't know why that's such a popular move, because I asked the question with the hopes of receiving an answer." The heaviness, courtesy of depression, is making my eyes droop, and the longer I sit, the harder it will be to get up.

Dr. Wilson nods and glances to the door. "Ok. We don't have to talk about it, but I'm going to have to notify your parents." I nod. "I believe Dr. Webber is waiting for you. You're free to go." My muscles tremble when I push myself off the couch, and we walk out of the office in silence.

The mechanical click of the lock, like a stream of data in

my brain, makes my feet move forward into the unit. When I first came here, I remember Dr. Wilson joking about how much fun this game of psychological cat and mouse would be.

Sorry to disappoint, Wilson, but there's nothing to chase. This mouse is dead.

Chapter 23

When I met with Webber, I didn't say anything. I don't think I was there long enough to warm the chair. His face was graver and more concerned than ever.

The pen never moved.

I left him empty of notes and boiling over with worry, but none of it matters anymore. My first instinct was to head to my room, but then I remembered it was locked. Instead, I've been pacing the common area. I don't think twice about it, just that I need to keep moving. My heart is beating so fiercely the sound smacks my ears with urgency, racing alongside my thoughts.

Every step I take makes my legs quiver. The tops of my thighs burn and ache as if I've been going up stairs. When I raise my hand to brush away a loose strand of hair, my arm shakes. I've already had two 16oz cups of water, but my mouth is a desert. The saliva is viscous and sticky; my tongue feels like sandpaper. My head is prickling alongside the orchestrated bodily dysfunction ravaging me.

Anthony walks over to me, hands in his pockets. I keep pacing, but he intercepts me. "Why don't you take a seat?"

I cross my arms. "I've been sitting all morning." I move past him, but he follows.

"Cut the BS." The comment catches me mid-stride. "You never sit if you can help it. What do you think would happen if you did?"

Heat flushes my face, and I scoff, "Nothing. Look, *you* don't have to live here against your will. You could walk outside and no one would stop you. I can pass the time sitting and staring at the wall, or moving and staring at the wall. Call it a personal preference."

Anthony chuckles. "Let me know when you're done deflecting. I can wait." He crosses his arms, making him look like an ad from *Men's Health*. I consider walking away, but there's nowhere to go. Besides, if I don't finish this now, it will only get bigger.

"What do you want me to say? Some deep, personal explanation for my avoidance of chairs? There's nothing more to say."

He sighs and looks at me with a seriousness I didn't know he possessed. "You need to sit because even though you think you're exercising by pacing around the room, the only thing you're doing is killing your health. Your blood pressure was low this morning, so I know it's probably hard to stand. Maybe you're dizzy or feeling weak, but you're walking anyway. So when every part of your body wants and needs to sit, you choose to stand. Eating disorders like to do that. But you don't have to listen, Willow." He sits down and pats the chair next to him. "Take a seat."

I glare at the empty seat with as much contempt as I can muster. Anxiety makes my skin itch from standing still. "I need to get something from my room."

He shakes his head. "Let's chat first." Looking across the room, there aren't any other nurses available, so this is my only chance. I cross my arms, swallow my pride, and sit on the very edge of the seat. I keep my posture ridged, but within seconds my back starts to ache and tremble.

"You can relax, you know." I keep my spine stiff and stare out the window as if Anthony hadn't spoken. "So, here's the thing. I know you've probably heard this several times by now, but you have to stop this, Willow. You have to acknowledge what you're doing to yourself. And I don't just mean the self-harm." This gets my attention. I turn to face him, and he returns my gaze, unflinching. "Yeah, I know about that. Did you think we wouldn't notice the limp? I wanted to give you the chance to come clean first, but this is something I have to report. A female nurse will have to take a look at it."

I narrow my eyes and shake my head. "I pulled a muscle when we went sledding. You weren't there, so you didn't see it happen."

Anthony doesn't so much as blink. He retorts, "I thought we were going to cut the BS? I've been working here for five years, and I've met much better liars. You need to see that your eating habits are *killing you*."

There's a rising, growing storm of tumult inside me, gathering mass. I want to scream, bust through the window and run straight into the cold and never stop. I want to cut and feel the way I used to feel when emptiness meant happiness, not heaviness. I want to be so light that not even the ceiling can hold me back, but my limbs feel so heavy I might as well sink through the floor.

But I don't say anything. Antony continues, "I see how you look at food like it's poison. I know that underneath that disgust is actually fear. Maybe you're afraid of what the food means once you eat it, and maybe you're afraid that if you start eating, you won't be able to stop." He lets this sink in. I try to wear indifference like armor, but his comments cut right through the warped steel.

I look back out the window, but I can feel Anthony's gaze on the side of my face. "I know that right now that voice inside your head is screaming at you to keep moving, because resting feels like failure. I've gotten to know you since you've been here, so I know that when I see you now, someone else is telling you what to do. Your eating disorder is distorting your entire perspective. You used to read books like you could live on them alone. When was the last time you touched a book?"

I'm dimly aware that my chest is moving fast. In and out, in and out, like I can pump all the blackness from my lungs. Maybe there's some truth to Anthony's words, but the beauty in being in a place so far gone, is that no one can reach me. *Don't listen to him. You're not thin enough to have an eating disorder anyway.*

A smile creeps across my lips, splitting my face. "Well, thanks for the chat. Can we go to my room now?" I stand up and crack my knuckles. Anthony gives a small sigh and stands.

"You don't have to talk to me, but you're going to have to talk to someone, just so you know." We walk out of the common area, down the hall in silence, and stand in front of my door. Anthony takes out his keys and unlocks the door. He stands in the frame while I go inside, not willing to take any chances, apparently.

I pad across the room, frantically scanning for something

to suit the lie of needing to be here. He won't leave me here unaccompanied, and I can only get in with the help of staff, but what if the door isn't locked?

I crouch beside my bed and select a random book from the haphazard pile, glancing at the time on my nightstand clock. Five minutes after checks. I should have enough time. "Find what you need?" I pop up, waving the book.

"Yeah, just trying to find the last one I haven't read." My jab makes Anthony shake his head, and I rejoin him by the door. He stands statuesque while I shuffle out of the room, thinking fast. I scuff my foot on the floor, and the other snags the toe of Anthony's shoe.

In one fluid, theatrical move, I go flying to the floor, letting the book soar out of my hand and up the hall. "Willow!" Five delicate fingers loop around my arm as he pulls me up. "Are you alright? What happened?"

I yank my arm away and shake my head. "I *tripped*. I never pretended to be graceful." Anthony's eyes narrow as he scans me over, and I can practically see the gears turning, wondering if this is somehow an elaborate lie. I sweep a conveniently stray hair out of my eyes and brush nonexistent dirt from my pants.

Apparently satisfied, he strides over and crouches down to retrieve my book, which somehow flew ten feet away of its own volition. Physics is funny that way.

I take a half step back, wait for Anthony to stand, and pull the door shut. The latch catches on the jam, but doesn't click all the way. As long as it rests on the frame, I don't need to turn the handle to get in. Anthony watches me, and I roll my eyes. With a defeated march, I take the book from him and walk back into the common area.

He takes an empty seat behind the nurses' station, none the wiser. I select the chair farthest away, flip open the pages, and smile to my company of words. They are the only witnesses to my psych hospital crime, and boy, does deception taste good.

I groan internally as Zena pokes my arm, and we crowd the door for lunch. "Where have you been? I know Tuesday groups suck, but the rest of us still go."

My face hardens, and I step away from her. "Well good for you. Make sure you get all your gold stars in the nut house." I laugh dryly, roll my eyes to the ceiling.

"What's your problem?" Zena's expression is razor-sharp.

I hug my arms around myself and smile. "No problem here. Maybe you should check yourself."

Zena crosses her arms and sets her jaw. The anger is

almost palpable, like she's giving off an aura of heat. "Cut the shit. Why are you being like this?" The door buzzes open, and our huddle shifts forward. "Oh, I forgot, it's *lunchtime*."

A select few words rise from my throat but before they can roll off my tongue, Anthony calls, "Willow! Come here for a minute." Zena breezes past me, leaving a trail of honey-vanilla scent in her wake of fury.

I close my eyes in a moment of composure, then turn and raise my eyes to Anthony. *Please don't be about the door. Please be about some new insane rule from Wilson.* He's leaning against the nurses' desk, swinging a set of keys on a lanyard. "You're supposed to eat in the nutrition room for meals." Anthony holds up his hands as if to say, *don't shoot!*

I roll my eyes and look back at him. Behind me, the locks engage, audibly screaming that I'm screwed. Anthony returns my stare, swinging his keys around and around, completely unfazed. *Swish-cling. Swish-cling.* "I think I would rather read."

"You don't have to eat everything. We can get a replacement shake. Just try." A small sigh creeps through my tight lips. I look outside. I look into the cold, into the quietly falling snow. I look at the way individual flakes are caught in streaming sunbeams, at how beautiful things never try to be beautiful. I think of the pull I feel to that landscape of cold, and the memories hidden under the ice.

"If you let me go outside, then I'll try." My eyes stay fixed on the window. A pause expands between us, pulling me farther beyond the glass.

"Why do you want to go outside?"

I fire back, "Why do you want me to eat?"

Swish-cling. Swish-cling. "I want you to live, Willow."

Breathe in. Breathe out. "Then there's your answer." I can feel him studying me and turn to face him. His eyebrows are pulled in close, and his dimples stand out from pressing his mouth shut tightly. But it's his eyes. There's a desperation in them, a hope. And that right there is my ticket.

"Let me clear it with Lead." He dials the phone, and I close my eyes. *This is it. This is when I remember.* Tiny beads of sweat collect on my palms, but I don't wipe them off. This is happening. This is finally happening.

Anthony sets the phone back in the receiver with a jolting snap. "Five minutes. The deal is you have to eat at least 50% of your meal before you can supplement the rest."

I open my eyes, and the color melts away.

It's black and white. Steel and cold.

Swish-cling.

Thud-snap.

"Let's go."

Chapter 24

I'm numbly aware of walking through the locked doors, padding down the hallways. I can't believe this is happening. My stomach is tight with knots of fear. And I can *feel* it. My memory is a crocus, ready to bloom out of the snow and dazzle us all. Anthony and I reach the last set of doors, the ones I know are unlocked. He pushes open the door on the right, walks out, and holds it open for me. I take a breath, and walk outside.

The cold air hits my face first. It snakes under my nostrils, slithers down my trachea, and freezes my lungs. I take a tentative step on the sidewalk, and curtains of clouds close over the sun, turning the sky black. The air is thick with darkness, permeating everything. I take another step into the snow-covered grass, and a shiver racks my body. Snow starts to fall, grey specks in a dark night. My feet leave a trail, but wind covers the craters. I'm invisible.

The trees in front of me dissolve, and in their place is a building. It's tall and round, made of metal. A water tower. I walk closer to it and run my hand over a patch of rust.

There's an open ladder running up the side to the top, but twenty feet up it gets swallowed in blackness.

I wonder how high it goes.

I wrap my fingers cautiously around the ladder rungs, testing their strength. The metal is cold on my skin, colder than ice. My grip loosens and I breathe into my hands, but the hot air dissipates almost immediately. I set my left foot on the first rung, and it holds.

With a last look at the ground beneath me, I climb. Each new rung bites farther into my fingers. The higher I go, the windier it becomes. My fingers have gone from numb to painfully frostbitten, although it's too dark to be sure. My heart is hammering from the heights, because if I fall now, it won't work, but I'll be injured. There's a cramp in my left calf that sears every time I place it on a new rung. My thighs and arms are sapped of energy, like the cold sucked away their strength.

With each step I grunt in effort. The farther from the ground I go, the heavier I feel. I guess part of me thought my body would sense what's about to happen, like some superhuman surge of adrenaline would somehow keep me alive, but I guess it's given up, too. The cold air leaves my mouth tasting like iron, and my lungs prickle with each inhalation.

I swear quietly every time I have to use my left leg. The

pain shoots into my quad and down to my Achilles, and even when it's dangling, I can still feel it pulse and spasm. I look up the ladder, then down, and decide I have to be about halfway up. My forearms feel weak and overused, but somehow there's enough strength to cling to the bars.

I stretch out my right hand to the rung above me, lift up, and raise my left leg. The moment I set it down, my calf spasms, and my foot slips,

and my hands slide away,

and my body leans back,

and the snow falls like stars,

and I plummet soundlessly though the space, pushing through the snowflakes like a meteor blazing to earth.

And when I hit the ground, I realize there was never any whiteness. There were never any stars. Just disaster. Because there's nothing hidden in this memory but pain. Agony. Fire splitting apart my bones, puncturing a hole in my lung, tearing through arteries. The memory is a bubble of pain I just burst.

I climbed into the blackness, and fell into the white.

Chapter 25

"Willow? Can you hear me?" Anthony and Amanda are hovering over me, invading my room. I don't remember how I got inside, but here I am. The tip of my nose and my fingers are numb with cold, so I can't have been here long.

Every time I close my eyes, there's snow. Every blink is a frame of a movie I don't want to watch anymore. I don't know if I can handle this. In a day Dr. Wilson will employ "medical intervention". My memory is something better left buried, but now the door is kicked open, and the cold just keeps coming in. And I'm freaking *hungry*, but it's not a good thing anymore.

I look around the room and spot a tray of food on my desk. It feels like a million years ago that I left the door unlocked, planning to come back and exercise. I wrap my arms around myself, but I can't stop shaking. There's too much, just too much and I can't make it stop.

I think I've finally done it. I've lost, but this was never really a game. I was just playing myself, and I lost. I pull my knees to my chest, trying to keep myself together even though I'm completely unhinged. *This is it. You've finally lost it.*

Chapter 26

I've drown once before
In this black place

I can feel the water filling up my lungs
the paradoxical burning of
suffocation

I'm falling beneath the waves
down
to a place where light doesn't exist

I keep falling
down
into oblivion
someone

help me

I can't

breathe.

Chapter 27

There's so much to feel that I feel nothing. I'm sailing swift currents of dissociation, somewhere both here and nowhere. So I sit, watching snow illuminate in the sodium-filled lamps, feeling both everything and nothing.

My cheek presses against the cool glass until they are both the same temperature. I want to walk out into the night, feel my bare feet burn in the cold. I want to walk to someplace where there is snow and trees and sky, and nothing else. I want to lay down in the snow, stare at the stars, and let the frost take me away.

Someone, please, take me away.

Chapter 28

I'm sitting on the floor, rocking back and forth. My head hits the wall every time, but I don't stop, even through the soreness. I've been here for a while, I think. My toes have fallen asleep.

Everything *hurts*.

People come in to check on me, but I don't say anything. I don't have the energy. There's a coldness trickling down from my head, into my neck, drowning my lungs. Everything is *so cold*. It's inside me, in my organs and bones and blood, freezing from the inside out. The goosebumps on my arms stand on end, but I don't even shiver. My brain is resigned to heating a body too lethargic to ever be warm.

I can't escape the pain. It comes when I breathe, when I think, with every moment I'm still alive. It comes and comes and comes and I'm screaming and screaming and *makeitstop* but still it comes. I ran out of tears a long time ago. My mouth is open, my eyes shut tight, but eventually there is no air left in my lungs to scream.

Pain fills the void.

Sometimes I'm adrift for a few moments, floating away from myself like a ghost. In this space there is nothingness, a limbo between living and pain. But it always finds me. No matter where I go, it always finds me.

There are scratches all over my arms, but I don't remember making them. They should sting, but I can't feel them. Inside me every cell, every compound and element, every *molecule* is on fire.

Not many people know what it's like to be on fire. How at first, your skin turns red, begins to sweat. Then it bubbles and peels and smokes and the smell of your own burning flesh sears the receptors in your nose. The pain erupts as raw nerve endings are exposed to the air, and everything is awash in inexplicable agony. You stand there, watching your skin smolder away.

But fire is only a metaphor. Because being burned by fire is easier to understand than the way frostbite slowly necrotizes the tissues in your body. With fire, the pain is acute, but frostbite is sadistic enough to make it *linger*. The pain is cold, depression cold.

I'm not sure how long I've been in this pain, but I can't remember *not* feeling it.

I can't imagine ever *not* feeling it.

I'm trapped in this body.

Someone

let me

out.

Chapter 29

"Willow." Someone's voice reaches my ears from far away. "When did these happen?" There are careful fingers on my wrists. Their touch is cool on my stinging skin. The lights are on in my room, but outside the window it's dark. Two more people walk in, and my arms get manipulated into bandages.

I look down at them in their brightly marked denotations: *crazy*. There's skin trapped under my fingernails. Two of the nurses walk out, but one stays behind.

Watching.

Chapter 30

I close my eyes. *Flash.*

Snowflakes caught in the moonlight.

Flash.

The silhouette of a building. I don't want to go, but something is pushing me forward.

Flash.

I'm at the bottom, staring at the top, wondering what the view will look like.

Flash.

Someone is grabbing my hands, peeling my fingers off the rungs. I don't want to fall; I don't want to do this. I don't want to do this. *I don't want to do this.*

Flash.

There's laughter, but it isn't mine. I realize I'm falling, and I'm terrified. This isn't what I want, but I can't stop it.

Flash.

My right arm hits the snow.

"Willow?" Amanda is grabbing my arm. "Are you ok?" My

room comes into focus, but everything is still blurry. Something hot trickles down my cheek, and it gets clearer.

I close my eyes, pray for empty blackness. My voice is hoarse, like I've been yelling. I croak, "Make it stop. It won't stop." Fresh tears slide down my face, and my head hits the wall. *Get it out.* My head hits the wall again, and again.

"Willow, calm down."

Thump.

getting it

thump

all

thump

out.

"I need some help in here!"

Chapter 31

There are drums

And yelling

Bodies moving too fast

hit each other

I am somewhere in the chaos

perhaps the middle

There is something red on my white shirt

but I think it was there before

Someone is crying, and it's the saddest sound I've ever heard

It's a guttural sound

like a dying animal

There's something sharp

then a burn

When my eyes close

the crying stops

Chapter 32

There is

                        Sound

Chatter.

Whirring, something is whirring.

Feet on carpet.

I hear whispers

                        Scared

Someone else's breathing

                        Labored

"Willow."

Whose voice?

"Willow."

                        A woman's.

"Wake up."

Wake up.

Wake up

                        Willow.

"She's been out for hours."

Get up

                        Willow.

Light from somewhere

Faces peering

I can't move.

Need to move

                        Willow.

"There you are."

Here I am?

A smile,

                        Amanda's.

It starts to

                        Hurt.

No, no, no.

Don't make it

                        Hurt.

I don't want it to

                        Hurt again.

Amanda

Make it

                        End

It won't

                        End.

Go to sleep

                        Willow
Make it end
                        Willow.
"Willow?"
Take it
                        Away.
Please
take it
                        Away.

Chapter 33

I think the word they're using is "setback". Maybe "episode". No one talks about it in the past tense, not yet. I'm sitting on the floor again with my knees pulled tight to my chest. Shivers ripple though me so that my teeth chatter endlessly. My neck and shoulders ache with it, taut and frozen in place. I feel feverish with pain. Even my bones ache now, a deep, deep ache in places I never knew could hurt.

The nurses who watch over me usually try to make conversation for the first part of their shift, but it always ends in mutual silence. "How are you feeling, Willow? How about a walk around the unit?"

"Are you hungry, Willow?"

"You need to eat, Willow."

"This isn't good, Willow."

I never reply. I've finally been swallowed whole by this thing. The black, tarry thing isn't just inside me anymore, it *is* me. My motions are slow, fighting the viscous rubber. Even breathing takes more energy than I have; it just takes too much effort to make my ribcage move an inch through the tightening bonds.

I think most people know hopelessness, but in a conceptual way, like reading the definition from a dictionary. They picture what it would feel like to have a complete absence of hope, but I don't think they can, not really. Somewhere in their minds, in some buried fissure, tucked away for better comprehension, hope lingers on. How can someone understand sickness when they are healthy, understand pain when they are whole?

But in all of this, the pain isn't the worst part. It's the hopelessness. The pain is just a qualifier. Because I was in pain yesterday, and the day before. I was in pain before I got here. I was in pain before the school year started, or the actual year started. So what's to say that I won't be in pain tomorrow? Or the next day, or the next year?

This is hopelessness. There's a story in Greek mythology about a titan named Prometheus. He is most famous for stealing fire from Olympus and giving it to man. But Zeus didn't like this, and sentenced Prometheus to an eternal punishment. Every day, while chained to a rock, an eagle would swoop down and eat Prometheus's liver. Being immortal, it would regenerate overnight, ready to be plucked apart again the next day. And the one after that, for eternity.

Or Sisyphus, since the Greeks love stories of hopelessness. Doomed to push a boulder up a hill only to have it roll to the bottom, sitting in wait to climb the hill again. And again. Because anyone can withstand any amount of discomfort, or even agony, so long if it is temporary.

Amanda, the nurse assigned to me this shift, repositions herself in the chair. She's reading a book, just to be ironic, on child and adolescent psychiatry. It looks like something straight from Webber's shelf: "10th Edition with all new approaches for complex cases and targeted therapies." It sounds like a politician met psychology, fancy and vague.

A knock on the doorframe makes me flinch. It's too early for lunch, and not time for a new watchdog. And, well *shit*, Webber walks into the room, hands in his pockets, and a frown between his eyebrows. *Not good.* He approaches Amanda's chair, who looks at him with rapt attention. "I wanted to have a chat with Willow. Do you have the latest report?" She leans over the side of the chair and pulls out a clipboard.

Amanda shuffles a few papers and plucks one free. "It's here," she says, handing it to Webber. He squints at it, eyes flicking over the writing faster than I can blink, and hands it back to Amanda. I almost want to shout, "Hello! Right over here!", since I'm betting the "report" are Amanda's notes on my doing absolutely nothing. She dog-ears a page in her book and stands up. "I'll be at the nurses' station when you are finished." Amanda smiles at me and walks from the room.

Leaving me with Webber. He doesn't take Amanda's chair, instead Webber sits on the foot of my bed, facing my corner of shame. I wait for him to say something, but again he moves to contradict me, allowing silence. His presence makes my bubble of quiet feel like a prison, and I shift my gaze out the window, wishing I could dissolve through the glass.

He lightly taps his fingers, politely waiting, and remains silent. I watch him out of my periphery, looking around at the room like I do in his office. My back starts to hurt, but I don't want to break the tension, so I stay still. A bird flies to a snow-laden tree branch. Bits of dead shrubbery poke out through the powder from the ground. Webber is so quiet that I wonder if he's breathing.

I would take Amanda back, right now. Someone to break this thickness. Someone to fill in my share of words, because there isn't a conversation Webber could steer that would be good. The silence worms its way through me, wriggling feelers of anxiety at each point of contact. My muscles are so ridged that my shoulders and calves start to twitch and cramp.

Webber seems perfectly content with my discontentedness. In a motion of defeat, I stretch out my legs, repositioning my body to restore the blood flow. The tension streams out from my muscles, and I relax into the wall, my fight gone.

"Well," I concede, "this has been a great chat. Let's call it a day." Webber chuckles and runs a hand through his hair.

"How are you doing?"

I shrug. "Fine."

"Do you know what 'fine' stands for?" I shake my head. "Freaking out, insecure, neurotic, and emotional."

"Well then, like I said. I'm fine."

He folds his hands in his lap and smiles. "So what are you freaking out about?"

I roll my eyes. "Maybe the medical threats looming over my head, or the fact no one will even talk about when I can go home."

"Nice deflection, but try again."

I sigh and give him a look of desperation. "I don't know. I don't know what happened."

Webber tilts his head just slightly and pinches his eyebrows together. "Tell me what you do know."

I smooth my palms against my legs and take a steadying breath. "I…remembered something. Or I thought I did." He nods encouragingly. "It was the night I…the time when…" I look at Webber, plead with my eyes that he can say the words, but he stays quiet. "When I jumped. But it was different."

"Different how?" Webber's voice is soft, but there's a palpable thickness in the room.

"I'm not sure. It didn't feel like I was alone."

He nods and asks, "Who else was there?"

"Well, no one. It was just me. But my thoughts…it was like something else was telling me what to do." I close my eyes, swallow my fear, and dive back into the night. There's a voice whispering in my ear, pushing me on with each rung. *You deserve this. Everything is your fault. You'll never be enough.* I remember it was so cold because I didn't wear a coat. Partly because I didn't see the point, but also to make my body work harder. Even then, even walking to the end, Ed was there, calling the shots.

"What do you remember?" I open my eyes and immediately find the window. The sky is clear again, but a thick layer of snow covers everything.

"I felt like I failed."

"Failed who?" I meet Webber's eyes. He knows exactly what I'm talking about, but he waits for me to say it.

"My eating disorder."

Chapter 34

I stab my fork into a pile of depressed-looking mashed potatoes. "Do I really have to?" Anthony gives me a knowing look and nods. The plastic grows slick in my hand, and I scoop up a small amount.

"Bigger bites."

I scowl at him. "Seriously? Eating is eating."

He counters, "And you're still trying to maintain control by taking tiny bites." I stare back at the plate and load up my fork with the lukewarm mush. *Don't do it! How are you going to get rid of it? You're pathetic!* "You've got this, Willow." I lift the fork to my mouth. The starchy, buttery smell hits my nose, making me want to gag. I shove the food into my mouth and chew slowly.

The same moment my taste buds send off fireworks, anxiety sends off a bomb blast. I swallow the potatoes and gulp down the entire cup of water. *Do you know what you just ate? Do you know everything that was in that single bite?* I shove the tray away and push my chair back. Anthony coaches, "I know this is hard, but you're doing great."

I run my hand frantically over my hair and glance to the door. "I can't do this. I'm sorry."

"Do you want me to get a replacement shake?"

I start pacing small circles around the chair. "Yeah. Wait no. I don't know. I don't think I can do this."

Anthony speaks calmly. "It's ok. You *can* do this. We'll take it one step at a time." I nod and glance again toward the door. "First thing is to sit down." I look at the chair and a new wave of anxiety washes through me. *It's a freaking chair, just sit down.* But sitting down means the mashed potatoes will actually get digested, means I can't pace away the single bite.

I grab the seat-back, take a breath, and sit. "Good. If the mashed potatoes are too difficult, you can try the applesauce. I know the choices aren't great, but you have to reintroduce food to your body slowly."

I agree absentmindedly. "Right. Ok." The cup of applesauce already has the top peeled off, so no nutritional label. I dip a spoonful in my mouth and swallow. Then another. *This sucks.* When I get to the end, I spread the applesauce around the sides.

"Nope. You have to eat all of it." Anthony is a *hawk*.

"It's empty. It's done." I tip the container to him in proof.

"Before I came here, I worked in an eating disorder facility. I know all of the behaviors." I toss him a glare and scrape the edges. With a final bite, I swallow the applesauce in exaggerated, sarcastic motions. At last, it's empty. I glance at the clock; it took me half an hour to eat *applesauce*. "Nice job. I'll swap the rest for a shake."

"Can I go back to my room?"

He shakes his head. "Sorry, got to make sure that food stays in your stomach. Besides, you're going to need blood drawn in a couple hours to make sure your body can cope with the food." This day keeps getting better.

For the next half-hour, I work on the shake under the constant watch of Anthony. When I'm finally done, I join Zena and Emerson on our favorite moldy couch in the common area. Zena is attempting to braid Emerson's short, choppy hair and glances up when I approach.

Smiling, Emerson pats the empty cushion. "Take a seat, darlin'." I lean into the arm rest and curl into the cushions.

Zena shakes her head and laughs. "Em, there's no way. Hand me that hair-tie." She twists a lock of hair at his crown and leaves it sticking in the air. "There you go. That's a good look on you." Emerson reaches up and wraps the hair around his finger.

"Ah, you know me so well. Thanks, babe." We fall into an easy silence. Zena pulls out a book, and Emerson and I hang out in the quiet. I lean my head back and close my eyes.

Colors swirl in the blackness from the flickering blubs. The image fades into dots of twinkling lights. As I watch them, the lights peel away from their black sky, flitting to the ground like fireflies. An imaginary breeze sends them whirling into snowflakes, falling and swaying and tumbling through the air, but never reaching the ground.

Is everything I've done tainted by this eating disorder? Does every thought, emotion, and action belong to something else? Who am I if all of this isn't me? I think back to life before Glenview, sift through the hazy memories in search of anything authentic. Everywhere I look it's there, lurking in the background. I picture it like a ghost that only shows up in photographs, impossible to see head-on.

And in each album of memories I reel back, that black, translucent shape is there. The farther back I go, the less substantial it becomes. When did this start? Was it there for the middle school mixer I was too afraid to attend? Was it there in elementary school when I graduated from extra small to small and cried? How can I possibly form an identity if I get rid of something that's been with me through everything?

"Hey, Emerson?" He turns his head to face me, bouncing the piece of skyward hair.

"What's up?"

"Do you think you'll ever not have bulimia?" He doesn't answer immediately and stares pensively at the TV.

"I don't know. I mean I know people recover, but I don't know if it totally goes away."

"What do you mean? Aren't they the same thing?" I rub my thumb into the palm of my other hand, something my mom does when she's stressed.

"People stop listening to their eating disorder, but I think it takes a long time to stop hearing it. But hey," Emerson says, waiting for me to meet his eyes, "it *does* get better. That I can promise. It might not always seem like it's worth it, but it totally is. Once you hit that first day when things seem easier, not perfect, but easier, you find out exactly why you're choosing recovery, and it's amazing."

I nod and stare at the blank TV. How is fair that this boy has already lived so much? He always seemed so easygoing, but under that is some serious emotional scar tissue. I hope it heals, one day. Zena interjects, "Hey guys?"

"What is it?" Emerson is the first to react.

Zena looks down at the carpet and back up, filled with tears. Emerson grabs her hand and a single tear tips over the edge. "I'm leaving. Tomorrow."

The words tumble from my mouth. "What? When did you find out?"

"Yesterday, during therapy." Zena sniffs. We all look at one another, caught between joy and sadness. "It sucks, right? I mean Fridays are our *day*. But Dr. Wilson said he and my parents talked about it last week, they just didn't say anything."

"Hey," Emerson soothes, "you are going to be *fabulous*. And you'll have our numbers so we can all stay in touch when we get out."

Zena nods, sending a second tear racing down her face. It strikes me that she's also someone who's had too much life in too little time. "You too, Willow?"

"Of course! Think of what life will be like with actual phones instead of walkie-talkies."

She chuckles and shakes her head, sending her icy-blond pony-tail swishing side to side. "Hey, those things are like gold here."

"Touché." Emerson giggles to himself, and both of us look at him skeptically. "You good?"

He comes up for air. "Yeah, yeah. You know, for the longest time I thought it was 'tooshie'."

"Oh yeah?" I give him a sassy look. "And when was that? Last week?" We let laughter wash over us like ignorance and wear it comfortably for the rest of the day. Our happiness may be temporary, but for now, we bathe in it. When life sucks in general, it can be scary to let in anything good, because inevitably, it will end. But now I see these moments are the ones worth living for, like Emerson said. One day they won't just be moments.

It's not possible to look forward to family therapy, but I'm at least dreading it a shade less. Maybe because it's on a Friday since my freak-out (just as Emerson predicted) pushed everything back a day, or maybe because nothing can get any worse than it already has. I can practically feel myself glowing with optimism.

I knock on Webber's door. "Come on in." The office is cramped with heat, and I sit on the cool leather chair. Webber has his coat hanging off his chair and rolled up his sleeves to his forearms. "How are you?"

I start to say "fine", but backtrack immediately. "I'm good." I almost correct my grammar, but leave it as an act of rebellion. Crazy, I know.

Webber nods and rolls his infamous pen absentmindedly. Uh-oh. "Today's session is going to be a little different. Instead of having therapy with your dad, we're going to bring both parents in."

"Um, ok." As in *Webber, I'm not a fan of the suspense*. He dials the phone, and we sit in anxious silence. At least, my silence is anxious.

"Hello?"

"Hi, Marissa. It's Dr. Webber here with Willow. Let me get David on the phone." Webber dials my father's number, and he picks up on the third ring.

"This is David."

"Hi, David. I'm here with Willow and Marissa for today's session." Webber turns to face me, and I almost explode with anxiety. "I spoke with your parents recently about your treatment so far. It's the opinion of all the staff that you are no longer a danger to yourself." He pauses, and I nod. Where is this going? "We are arranging for you to be discharged a week from today."

What? How is this possible? Just a few days ago they were threatening to send me to the hospital. Excitement rises in me, but I push it back down. There has to be a catch here. "I'm going home? Just like that?"

Webber's mouth twitches down almost imperceptibly, snagging on that unsaid truth. "You'll leave Glenview next Friday and get transferred to a facility that specializes in eating disorders."

"I thought you said I was fine?"

Webber sighs and looks at me apologetically. "You aren't an immediate danger to yourself, but your eating disorder needs treatment beyond what we can give you here."

I rub my hand into my temple, trying to massage out my reeling thoughts. "But I'll be able to go home." Silence. "*Right?*"

My parents, apparently cowards, let Webber do all the talking. "Just a few days ago you self-harmed. While we don't believe you are suicidal, the severity of your eating disorder combined with the fact you are still relying on self-harm means that inpatient, at least right now, is the best next step."

My mom adds, "The place we found for you is a step-down treatment center. So after a little bit, you'll be able to come home and just go during the day." She says this like it's good news, like I should be thanking her.

"But," I plead, "I'm not like those other people. I'm not some emaciated model."

Webber jumps in. "Eating disorders aren't diagnosed based on how people look. They don't discriminate based on size, gender, race, or anything else. Eating disorders are *mental* illnesses with physical manifestations, Willow."

How is it when I get good news it still ends up bad? "Dad, do you agree with this?" It's a cheap shot, since I'm banking he doesn't buy into the whole "eating disorder" thing. To him, it's just me finally "applying myself".

"From what I'm hearing, this transfer is a necessary step in your treatment."

Anger flares up and shoves aside my anxiety. "Can you talk to me like I'm actually your daughter and not a client?"

He protests, "Willow, that's not—"

"—and why don't you say what you actually think instead of not wanting to go against the popular opinion. I *know* you think this is a waste of time, but you're just saying what's expected."

Webber interjects, "Let's all just take a second. Willow, I know this isn't the news you wanted to hear. What are you feeling right now?"

"What do you think I'm feeling?" I mutter, "This is ridiculous." I pick a piece of lint from my pants, thinking. "What if I got better, started eating more? Would I still have to go?"

The expression on Webber's face is grim. "Unfortunately, yes. These things don't just go away that quickly, under sheer willpower."

I set my mouth, run a hand through my hair, and look squarely at Webber. "So this is it. I don't get any say in what happens to me." Truth works its way through our silence. How can they possibly know what's best in my life when they aren't the ones living it? And just like that, any fallacy of control I thought I had over *my own life* is gone. "Well then, I'm not sure why you need me here. It looks like you guys have it all figured out just fine."

I push out of the chair and twist the doorknob. Anger rips through my veins like a drug. I'm getting transferred. Zena is leaving. *You know how to make this go away.* My feet propel me down the girls' hallway. It doesn't matter if someone catches me exercising, because what are they going to do? The wheels are already in motion.

I stop in front of the door and yank on the handle, but it doesn't budge. I try it again, but the door stays locked. "Are you kidding me?"

"Willow?" I close my eyes and lean my forehead into the door. Amanda. "Is there something you need?"

"Why is my room still locked?" I watch Amanda's eyes grow big and sad. She tips up her eyebrows and tilts her head, oozing false sympathy. "Of course." I walk past her, curling my hands into fists, back into the life everyone else demands on living.

Chapter 35

Zena left about an hour ago. It was relatively quiet, which was unlike Zena, but she left with tears in her eyes. This place is funny like that. Zena was probably brought here kicking and screaming, and I know she hated Glenview, but she was still upset over leaving. Friendships form fast and deep in places like these.

I've been mentally counting down the hours until dinner. There's a battle waging in my brain, and I can't tell which side I'm on. Part of me knows that I want to be free of this eating disorder, and actually eating would be a good step toward achieving that. But the other part of me wants to say *screw it*. There's too much happening right now, just too much tumult to think about eating.

I sit in the beanbag by the window and gaze at the snow. Icicles hanging from the roof drip away onto the pavement. The snow looks hard and crystalline as sunbeams strike it, bringing with it notes of springtime. I have a feeling winter keeps a firm grasp over these mountains.

My mind wanders to the facility I'm getting shipped off to. What part of the country will it be in? Will there be snow? It's a bit ironic, but I think I'll miss the snow. There's something different about this mountain snow than the grey, smog-filled Michigan snow. There's something alive, vital about it.

In the back of my mind, the clock ticks closer and closer to zero. My palms start to sweat as I imagine sitting across from Amanda, demanding more from every bite. "Lunch time, everyone!" One of the temp nurses calls everyone to the doors, and I sink lower into the beanbag. *I'm not here. No one can see me.*

Anxiety works over my muscles like an electric current, making them contract and freeze in place. *No, no, no. I can't do this.* "Willow? Are you ready for lunch?" The sound of Amanda's voice makes me jump.

"Yeah, sure." I get up slowly and follow her to the nutrition room, and I swear my heart beats quicker with each step. Thinking about it, it probably does since I'm dehydrated. She sticks the key into the handle and holds the door open for me. I step inside.

Amanda lets the door swing in behind her and takes the seat opposite me. A tray laden with food separates us like a division of wills. *Don't do this. Don't make that mistake again.* Webber told me this was the eating disorder voice, which apparently I'm supposed to visualize in the third person. But how can I be sure? It all sounds the same. I cross my arms and stare at the tray.

"How are you doing, Willow?" Amanda is a picture of concern. The anxiety courses through my blood, because *food* gives me a fight or flight reaction, which I find ironic. The decision is a clear one: flight.

"I'm still really full from breakfast, actually." I watch her smile grow warm and her eyes become firm.

"Why don't you just start with the apple."

I wring my hands in my lap. "I'm just not used to eating like this. I'm still full from this morning."

Amanda nods, and her smile holds. "I get that. Let's start small. Why don't you try the apple?"

Fear turns to anger. I clench my fists and push my seat back resolutely. "I'm not eating the fucking apple, ok?" The word tastes bitter in my mouth. The only other time I swore was when Brian accidentally gave me a black eye the day before school pictures. Now I'm cursing over *apples*.

Amanda leans forward in her seat. "Do you know what a nasogastric tube is?"

"Not sure that I want to."

She points to her nose. "It's a tube that goes through your nose, down your throat, and into your stomach. It's used for temporary feeding. It's also what's going to happen if you miss a meal." *This* was what Dr. Wilson meant by "medical intervention"? I thought he just meant an IV or vitamins.

"Look, I'm going to another place after this anyway next week, so it's not going to matter if I miss a meal."

She smiles even wider. "I'm aware that you're getting discharged soon, and that's so exciting! It doesn't mean, unfortunately, that you can skip any meals between now and then. I know this isn't fun, but you need to take care of your body."

I look at the apple skeptically. "If I eat the apple, can I substitute the rest?"

Amanda's smile might as well split her face in two. She nods and agrees, "Absolutely. I'm really proud of you, Willow."

I pick up the apple and bite out a chunk. For the next 45-minutes, it's just the three of us: Amanda, me, and the food. She watches every bite enter my mouth, encouraging me when Ed starts taking control. And for the first time in my memory, when I finish the apple, then the shake, I feel good. I like this kind of rebellion.

F-you Ed!

Somehow the weekend went by incredibly fast. Outings are off the table for me, but Emerson decided to stay back, so we hung out and played cards. Today is my last session with Webber. Emerson and I try to keep it light, but with Zena gone and me leaving, I can see the fear creeping into his mannerisms. This isn't a place you want to be alone.

"How much longer do you think you have?" I turn to Emerson sitting across the couch, watch his smile wane.

"I don't know. I've talked to my mom about it, and I think we're aiming for next week. My adventure to nowhere definitely didn't help."

I poke his foot with my shoe. "That's not too bad. Will you go back to school?"

"I guess. It's a little into the semester, but I won't have too much to catch up on."

I nod. "True." He wriggles his toes and pokes my foot back. I smile and lean back into the cushion.

"You going to therapy?" I move my foot and evaluate for a counterattack.

"Don't remind me. Any chance I'm not here?" Emerson laughs and doges my strike. I stand up, but he taps my arm.

"Here." There's a flash of red, and he shoves the Jolly Rancher in my palm. "I promise they taste even better when you eat them." I give him a sassy look and walk down the hallway, slipping the candy into my pocket. My eyes trace patterns in the carpet, finding a train of well-worn tracks through the middle. I trace a finger along the wall, letting the smooth paint wear down any nervous fluttering.

"Come on in." The door is already open, and Webber is at his desk, looking attentive. The pen is gone. I take a seat, for the last time, in that too-comfortable chair. I tuck my feet under the chair and rest my hands against my legs. "I know this is our last session, but you are free to talk about anything you would like."

Shame tries to hold my words back, but I dig up a wisp of courage and push them out. "I'm a little worried about this new place." Webber nods, and I continue. "I don't really think I belong with a bunch of girls competing to be the smallest. Wouldn't sticking a bunch of people with eating disorders together make it worse?" The nurses keep calling my eating disorder different things: anorexia, OSFED, which apparently is some catch-all, BS category.

"Eating disorders do tend to be competitive, but the other kids there are the people who understand most what you're going through. What did you think about Glenview before coming here?"

I shrug. "I guess." How long are they going to stick me there? Why do they think having to completely start over is the best path?

Webber tilts his head. "Is there something else on your mind?"

I roll the fabric of my pants between my fingers. "I get why thinking about the suicide attempt was hard. But I still can't think about the hospital. I kind of thought that when I remembered what happened, everything would change. That maybe things would get easier."

Webber leans forward and brings his hands together. "Willow, you went through a trauma. Many people find that the aftermath of a crisis is just as impactful. You woke up in the hospital faced with the consequences of your actions. You had to face your family, your friends. People probably asked you *why* several times a day, when maybe you didn't have the answer yourself. Trauma doesn't just go away. Remembering what happened that night is an important step, and it is still going to take a lot of time and patience for those memories to get any easier."

I nod and shift my gaze to the books behind his desk. "What about school?"

Webber asks, "How do you mean?"

"Well, I haven't exactly had perfect attendance. Do I have to go back?" My skin feels tight at the thought of having to return to school, to go back to that wasteland of isolation.

Webber weighs his answer. "The treatment center you'll be going to is close to your home. Your parents are in contact with your school to get all the missing work. I understand that once you get caught up, you have the option to complete the semester working with a tutor from home."

"Ok." I glance at the clock above the door: almost lunchtime.

"How do you feel about going back to school?"

A laugh bursts through my mouth. "I think I'll stick with the tutor." Webber smiles.

"Understandable." He watches me watch the clock. "The staff notes say that you have been eating more of your meals."

I shrug. "There's not exactly an alternative." A small groove moves between Webber's eyes.

"Give yourself some credit. I know it isn't easy, Willow, but you're pushing through your anxiety. How do you like shame group?"

Another laugh escapes me. "Like is a strong word."

"Well, eating disorders thrive on shame. Give yourself credit for pushing past those thoughts. Let yourself win." I nod, and Webber shoots another glance at the clock. "Well, it's about that time. I don't want to keep you from lunch." I roll my eyes, and he smiles.

Walking back down the hallway, I think this might actually be doable. Right now, things pretty much suck, and I know there will be setbacks, but, for the first time, I have hope.

Hope.

Chapter 36

"We'll meet up some time. We have to. Ok? It'll be ok." Emerson nods and leans in for a hug. I expect *"boundaries!"* to come soaring over our heads, but no one breaks us apart. I press my face into that fiery, curly mane of his and wrap my hands between his shoulder blades. "And you have my number. We can do this, Emerson. You'll be ok. You can make it."

We pull apart, and I watch his lopsided smile spread on that freckled face. "And you. You'll be *spectacular*, darlin'." I grin and punch him lightly in the arm.

"That's from Zena." He chuckles, looking over my shoulder to the place my parents stand. "You really saved me, you know. But you have to look out for yourself, too."

"Well, look who's full of wisdom." He jumps and puts a hand on my shoulder. "Just a minute. I almost forgot." Emerson spins on his heel and wheels down the boy's hallway. I turn to watch my parents slide predictably into their molds. My mom is chatting away with Amanda, gesticulating in that way only women can. My father, on the other hand, is standing awkwardly with his hands in his pockets, glancing around the unit. He reminds me of Jordan's parents.

Emerson comes jogging back into the room with one arm behind his back, grinning madly. "You asked, and I answered." He whips out a forest green beanie, presenting with his head bowed.

"Oh my god! How did you get it?" I examine it for authenticity.

"Ah, a magician never reveals his secrets." I punch him again, this time harder. "Ok, ok! I'll tell you next time I see you." I shake my head, smiling like a fool.

My suitcase stands waiting between my parents. "Well, I'll see you then. *Stay grand.*" I pull out my bun, putting the beanie snug over my ears. My dad looks up when I approach.

"Ready to go?" I nod. Amanda catches my eye.

"You'll do great, Willow. It was so good getting to know you while you were here." My mouth feels stuck with emotion, so I only nod. Amanda pats me on the shoulder and smiles.

My mom holds out my coat, but I shake my head. I need to feel the cold. I need to remember everything it took to get here, even the bad. We walk through the door; I don't flinch when the locks slide back into place.

Down the hallway, out the door, and into the sunlight we emerge with our backs to Glenview. My eyes gravitate to the snow. Poking out, instead of dead bushes, is a sparse, purple bloom. A crocus.

This isn't the story of a broken girl who falls in love and gets saved. This isn't the story of the friends that meet in a psychiatric hospital and cure each other. This is the story of a girl with a little too much sass who finds friendship in the most unlikely place, and discovers recovery in herself. In this story, there are lots of stars. Some shining boldly in the black sky, others twinkling like snow in the moonlight. I used to think there was only disaster, but now I see that there were always stars; sometimes they just hide behind clouds.

Made in the USA
Lexington, KY
06 October 2018